CHRISTMAS ON DEERY STREET

AND OTHER SEASONAL STORIES

Steven Roberts

Outskirts Press, Inc.
Denver, Colorado

Christmas On Deery Street And Other Seasonal Stories
All Rights Reserved.
Copyright © 2006Steven Roberts
v rl.0
Second Printing

Cover designed by Sandra Van Winkle

Outskirts Press, Inc.
http://www.outskirtspress.com

ISBN: 978-1-4327-1311-9

Library of Congress Control Number: 2006906599

Outskirts Press and the "OP" logo are trademarks belonging to Outskirts Press, Inc.

PRINTED IN THE UNITED STATES OF AMERICA

For my parents, Bill and Joy Roberts, whose lives inspired these stories.

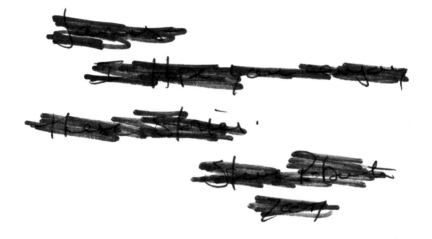

INTRODUCTION

I am fortunate to have grown up with a master story teller, my father. He told the same stories many times with many variations in detail. While each story in *Christmas on Deery Street...* is fictitious, there's a small element of truth that came from one of my dad's stories.

This book has been a long time coming. It would have never happened without the support of many people, more than I can name here. However, I would be terribly remiss if I did not recognize a few.

My sister and brother-in-law, Cathy and Len Willard; my brother and sister-in-law, Ramsey and Carolyn Roberts; and my children, Nick and Courtney, have all provided constant support and inspiration.

John Watson, my best friend and hero for over forty years, has been and remains my greatest fan and my toughest critic.

Nan Lillard, Allen Fethe, Debbie Roberts, and Ed Nicholson have encouraged me to write for years.

Colleen Goulet, my publishing representative at Outskirts Press, has been invaluable in helping me through the publishing process.

Janice Myers and Alyson Kennedy provided invaluable conceptual, critical, editorial, and organizational assistance.

Sandi Van Winkle designed the front cover and arranged the back cover, and provided many creative and artistic suggestions.

The Parables Class has allowed me to read my stories each Christmas and received them with enthusiasm and encouragement.

I will be forever grateful to all of those mentioned and not mentioned here. Without them this collection would have never happened

CHRISTMAS ON DEERY STREET

CHRISTMAS ON DEERY STREET

Everyone called him Blondie. Most didn't know why. They just assumed he had blond hair at some point in his life. But he never did.

Blondie was named Othello Lafayette Robinson, for his mother's favorite Shakespearean character and the famous French general. As a girl she loved to read but only had two books, which were her mother's — Shakespeare's *Othello* and a biography of General Lafayette. When Blondie came along, she wanted her firstborn to have a name of distinction.

His childhood friends had trouble saying his name. It was long and cumbersome and unusual, especially his first name. Most pronounced it O-the-lo. Ellen Colleen Moriarty, a fourth-generation Irish Catholic immigrant, labeled him Blondie. He loved to tell how he got his name.

***

All of the neighborhood kids used to sit on the huge, white marble stones that served as a retaining wall between our yard and the sidewalk. It was a natural sitting wall, especially in the summer, when the heavy stones provided the only cool place from the late-July heat. We'd sit on the stones in our underwear for hours at a time. At night we'd tell ghost stories and catch lightning bugs in mayonnaise jars, so we could put them on our window sills and let them blink us to sleep.

One especially hot day I was sitting in my favorite spot on the wall, watching a new family move in across the street. I was six at the time. A caravan of beat-up Ford pickup trucks pulled up across the street. They were loaded far above the side rails with chests, appliances, and bed frames. Boxes of kitchen and household items, small tables, and mounds of clothing filled the inside of the truck beds. Each truck had at least one mattress draped across the roof of the cab and tied down from bumper to bumper. I was fascinated that so much stuff could fit into such small spaces. And as soon as one truck was unloaded, off it would go for another load.

After about three round-trips for each truck, two late-model Chevrolet station wagons pulled up, jammed with people and more boxes. Children literally fell out of the cars once the doors opened. They began running in and out of the house, until a loud female voice yelled, "Everyone stop! Into the house, now!" From then on all moved with order, civility, and silence.

My safe little world was under siege. I would no longer be the king of the wall. The Moriarty's had arrived. All eleven of them. And in a few years, Billy and Jimmy Moriarty would introduce me to the virtues of tobacco and alcohol and pictures of women without their clothes on.

I had been watching the smallest, but not the youngest, of my new neighbors. She was shorter than me but appeared to be about my age. And she was the hardest worker of the bunch. She wore a bright yellow, sleeveless dress that made her look like a daisy with legs. She was barefoot. As I learned later, shoes were a necessary evil that were discarded as soon as possible.

She caught me looking at her and I felt like I had done

2

something I shouldn't have. As she walked across the street to lecture me on being a Peeping Tom, I wanted to run into the house, but feared that cowardice in the face of imminent danger would permanently harm my future manhood. So, I sat my ground and waited for my punishment. Deferring to what she had to say would be a big part of my life from then on.

I couldn't take my eyes off of her, as her bare feet moved with purpose and precision. Her arms swayed back and forth and made the sides of her dress move in syncopated rhythm. She stood right in front of me. I expected a lecture, but was amazed when she stuck out her hand and said, "I'm Ellen Colleen Moriarty. Nobody calls me Ellen Colleen except my mama when she's mad at me. So, if you know what's good for you, you'll just call me Ellen. Saw you looking at me. Figured you wanted to be friends."

I really didn't hear everything she said. Maybe I was mesmerized by her yellow dress. Maybe it was her curly red hair that fell to her shoulders. Or her moss-green eyes that were as big as silver dollars. I don't know. But from that moment, I was captured. I knew that she would be my best friend, my taskmaster, my cheerleader, my lifelong companion. She would inspire me to do things I could never have imagined. Find the best parts of me I never knew I had. Make me weep and rejoice because of her courage. And she knew it, too.

"What's your name? Can't be your friend if I don't know what to call you."

"O. L."

"What kinda name is that? Nobody has just letters for a name. Really, what's your name?"

"Othello Lafayette." I waited for her to start laughing, like all the kids did. But she just put her finger on her cheek, cupped her chin, and stood there thinking.

3

"That'll never do. Did your mother not love you or something? Were you an ugly baby? Why would she name you that?"

I just stood there with my head hung, feeling dumb.

"I know. I'll call you Blondie. I like that name. Yeah, Blondie it is."

The funny thing was, I didn't have blond hair. Never. Mine was as black as coal. She just made it up right there. Just like that. Nobody knew why, not even Ellen. From then on, I was Blondie; and I never questioned it, or her, something that would prove to be smart as I got older.

Ellen pretty much ran the family, which was fine with me. She liked being in charge. I liked that, because she was good at bossing others around, and I wasn't. She was passionate and demonstrative and compelling. Quick to defend people of principles. He loved the way she could be filled with righteous indignation, especially when it was directed at those who took advantage of the ignorant, the innocent, the lost. He was less forceful, less argumentative, preferring to avoid conflict and confrontation.

***

Christmas Eve on Deery Street was an event, one that involved the whole neighborhood. The tradition began because of their only son, the fourth of their seven children. Being devoutly Irish Catholic, Ellen named their six girls — Magdalene, Ester, Sarah, Mary, Naomi, and Ruth – for strong, courageous women in the bible. She named their son Franklin Abraham, after the two presidents whom she said had seen the country through its darkest days.

Frank was a really bright, really big boy; taller, heavier, stronger than others his age. His hands were extraordinarily large, as if they could wield a spike-driving sledgehammer as easily as his favorite Louisville Slugger. He was an imposing sight. Those who didn't know him were instantly intimidated. Those who knew him loved him because his heart was even bigger. He was forever championing the outcasts; those others made fun of, those who were always picked last or by default. His sisters would bring home stray animals. Frank brought home stray kids. Blondie loved to tell the story of how Frank started their Christmas Eve tradition.

***

Late one Christmas Eve afternoon, I was sitting in the chair next to the window that looked out over the front porch and into the street. Naomi and I were reading the paper. Actually, I was reading the paper to her. She would stand in the crook of my arm as I held up the paper. She'd ask, "What's this say, Poppie?" or "Who's that in that picture?" But we'd always end up with the funnies. Her favorite was *Little Orphan Annie*. Sometimes she'd squat down on my lap in front of the paper so she could see Annie and Sandy better. Sometimes she'd say, "Come on, Poppie Warbucks. Let's see what's happened to Annie and Sandy today." That's how she learned to read; every night, standing in the crook of my arm, one hand holding the edge of the paper, the other around my neck.

This particular Christmas Eve, Naomi and I heard two sets of feet clomping on the front porch. We recognized one set as Frank's. The other was unfamiliar. About the time she got down to see who it was, they burst in. Frank had another boy in tow by the sleeve of his too-big corduroy coat.

Before anyone could ask, Frank blurted out, "This is my new friend, Roger. He's visiting his grandpa on

Luttrell Street 'cause his grandma died last year and his grandpa doesn't have anybody to have Christmas with because everybody lives someplace else. But his grandpa had to work tonight and he was just sitting out on the walk by himself. So I asked him what he was doing out there, and he said he was just waiting for his grandpa but he wouldn't be home till late."

This whole time, Roger never looked up. He just looked at his shoes, which were tied with several broken shoelaces. His hands and face were dirty. He looked tired and frightened.

As Frank continued his exposé of Roger's brief, little life, Naomi reached over and lifted Roger's face. His right cheek had a red welt along his cheekbone and his right eye was puffy. We later found out that Roger had just come to live with his grandfather to avoid an abusive father. His smudged cheeks had tear tracks on them.

"Naomi, why don't you take Roger into the bathroom and help him wash his face and hands? Then see if there's not some milk in the fridge. Or maybe Mom might have some hot chocolate ready."

She took Roger's hand and without a word — and with that smile I both loved and dreaded, because she knew I couldn't resist it and because it would cast her spell on some boy someday who'd take her away from me — she and Roger went off to clean up.

"Frank, you stay here. Naomi can take care of Roger. I want to talk to you. How come you brought Roger home? Does his mom know he's here?"

"No, sir. His mom's not here. She's at their house in Alabama. It's just Roger and his grandpa, and his grandpa's at work. He was just sitting there, shivering and crying. I didn't want to say he was crying in front of him. It might hurt his feelings, and he looks like he's been hurt already."

"Why'd you bring him here?"

"'Cause everybody's gotta have a place to go on Christmas Eve."

From that moment on, Frank's admonition became the theme for every Christmas Eve — that everyone should have a place to go on Christmas Eve.

***

Roger bounced between his grandfather's house, his mother's house, and the Robinson's house, which is where he preferred to live. There, he was a member of the family. He would sometimes stay for months at a time. Sometimes years. He would sleep on a pallet made of quilts and pillows on the floor in Frank's room, which was a converted attic for the only male offspring in the family — except when Roger was there.

As Roger got older, his visits were less frequent and of shorter duration. He joined the army after graduating from high school. Ellen and Blondie both wrote him every week. He rarely wrote back. After he was discharged from the army, he visited briefly a couple of times. Then he disappeared. Every five or six years he'd call. Roger wasn't much for keeping in touch.

***

The word quickly spread among their Deery Street neighbors, then among neighbors on Luttrell Street, and Eleanor Street, and even streets that were just barely considered to be in the neighborhood. If you had no place to go or if you just wanted some company, 713 Deery Street was the place to be on Christmas Eve.

Over the years the Christmas Eve festivities grew into

the Christmas event. Six o'clock was always the appointed time. Folks would line up at the front door. As the tradition grew, the line got longer and longer, sometimes winding its way down the sidewalk and around the corner on Fifth Avenue. Most were neighbors; some weren't. But it didn't matter. Everyone was always welcome.

Blondie and Frank would greet them with a warm "Merry Christmas" and a firm handshake. Unfortunately for him, Frank always had to greet the old ladies who'd tweak his cheek and say things like "You're so sweet," or "What a big boy you're getting to be!" or "Don't you just look like your mother." It didn't matter how old he was — the same little old ladies would say the same thing every year.

Ellen and the girls would be busy keeping glasses and plates filled. And if any of the young men hung around the table too long, visiting with one of the girls, they'd get a look from her that shot daggers into their hearts. The girls would then hurry back into the kitchen, and the boys would quickly leave the room, if not the house. Ellen's reputation as a woman whose tongue and index finger could bring grown men to their knees, whimpering for forgiveness, was legendary.

In any given corner you could hear discussions about the sad state of affairs at city hall. Or all the juicy gossip fresh from the beauty parlor of the latest scandal to rock the neighborhood. There weren't many decorations in the house. The focal point was a floor-to-ceiling tree covered with homemade ornaments and what seemed to be thousands of multicolored lights. The house smelled of turkey and cranberries and warm apple cider and fresh coffee. But mostly it was a place filled with the warmth of the season, filled with the hope and anticipation that Christmas brings, and filled with people who truly enjoyed being with each other.

Blondie sat at the end of the dining room table that seemed to reach from room to room. It was made of wormy chestnut by the Pennsylvania Amish. It easily weighed five or six hundred pounds and was at least one hundred years old. Ellen's great-grandfather had won it in a poker game down on Front Street.

Front Street, which ran along the north bank of the Tennessee River, was where you could get anything you wanted. Anything. Especially those things the law and society said were illegal or immoral. And you could find some things on Front Street nobody wanted. The riverbank was lined with barges permanently moored. On the barges were a variety of structures that housed a variety of activities. All were examples of the seedier, lustier side of life. Ellen forbid even the slightest mention of Front Street in her house, although Blondie would occasionally wander around down there, "just to observe human nature," as he put it. No one spoke of his few Front Street excursions. For the last few Christmases, promptly at six o'clock he would assume his seat at the head of the table, just as he had done for so many years. Sitting there alone brought back so many things — memories so clear and exact they could have just happened.

There was the year that Frank and Roger thought it would be fun to put laxatives in the brownie pan when Ellen wasn't looking. That year, Santa brought surprises throughout the neighborhood.

There were several memories about Sarah, the daughter who always had a boyfriend and who fell in love with every boy who said he liked her. There was a standing bet to see if one boy could make it for two Christmases in a row. None had. Blondie said she'd grow up to be a serial marrier.

There was the year Frank was in the war and Ellen

stayed at Mass all Christmas Eve night, lighting candles and praying for his safe return. Or the year when Magdalene left home with her new husband and created the first permanent vacancy at the table. And the year Ellen died, seven weeks and two days before Christmas.

As he sat at the table remembering, without thinking he reached under the table and rubbed the carvings on the inside of the side panel. He smiled. They were the initials of Magdalene and her first boyfriend, which symbolized a rite of passage created quite ceremoniously and passed down from Magdalene to her siblings.

His name was Jake Vaughn. Every facet of her fifteen-year-old life was consumed with Jake Vaughn, a boy three years older. His name or initials were written on everything Magdalene owned — homework, notebook, sneakers, papers all over her bedroom walls, the bathroom mirror, the inside cover of her bible. Jake was everywhere.

He was a leader-of-the-pack type, the kind fathers feared and mothers hated. He had a leather motorcycle jacket and the motorcycle to go with it, a Harley Davidson Electra-Glide they always heard but never saw. He carried a pack of Lucky Strike cigarettes rolled up in the sleeve of his white T-shirt, which also revealed a tattoo that read "Born to Raise Hell." Oh, how she wanted her name to be surrounded by a heart, forever etched on Jake's upper arm.

They loathed the idea of their firstborn associating with an older boy who clearly has no ambition or social grace. Ellen rarely passed up an opportunity to express her displeasure about Jake. But they knew that if they forbid her to see him, she'd run straight to him and sneak around after him.

"He's just motorcycle trash," Ellen would say. "A hoodlum. He'll never amount to anything. Most likely wind up in jail before he's twenty, or shot dead by a policeman while robbing someone's home. Probably ours. Boys like him only want one thing from girls, you know, young lady. And he's too old for you."

It came to her during one of Ellen's dinner lectures about Jake ruining Magdalene's and the family's reputation. Magdalene had reached down to retrieve her napkin from off the floor. It was instantly obvious what she must do.

Since there was no way to permanently inscribe his name on her body, the next best thing, she thought, was to carve their initials on the underside of the dining room table. The table four generations of Moriarty women had owned. The table her mother loved and almost worshipped as the symbol of family strength and stability. The table where her mother unleashed her Irish temper and venom on poor, sweet Jake. It would be a double blow: one for true love, and one for defiance against her mother's dictatorial rule.

Blondie actually discovered the "M. R. loves J. V." a few months later, but he kept it to himself. The truth came out during one of the spring cleaning marathons. Ruth, the youngest, was assigned to clean the table from top to bottom.

"Mama, come quick! Look what's written on the table."

Ellen rushed to the dining room, horrified that someone would write on the table.

"Where? Where's the writing? I don't see anything." She was relieved to find that the tabletop had not been defaced.

"No, mama. Down here."

Ellen stooped down and found Ruth sitting under the table, pointing to the eternal abbreviations of her sister's undying love. Ellen just looked at the carvings. Ruth sat there, afraid to move. Since she was within her mother's grasp, she would be the recipient of her mother's wrath. Ellen kept staring at the initials. Ruth kept waiting for the famous eruptions from her mother, but when nothing happened she quickly scooted out the other side and ran to her room, where she'd be safely out of range. Ellen remained in her half-sitting, half-squatting position, staring at the letters for several minutes. Then she stood and went back to the kitchen. Nothing was ever said about the initials neatly carved in her table. Magdalene had won. She had beaten her mother, but she never knew it.

When she felt it was safe to leave her room, Ruth quickly and proudly spread the word of how she had lived to tell the tale of the Dining Room Table Massacre. As the word spread, each child was filled with the same courage and defiance that had prompted Magdalene to act. Over the years, they each carefully — and only when no one was in the house — performed the same ritual, etching theirs and their heartthrob's initials on the underside of the dining room table. Except for Sarah, who was banned from initialing the table after her third set was discovered.

***

As his children became adults, they all moved away and had families of their own. The Christmas Eve tradition began to wane. One by one, they stopped coming home for the holidays, opting to have Christmas in their own homes rather than travel to his.

Ellen had died a slow, agonizing death from cancer. While it robbed her of her strength and her red tresses that reached to her waist and that she wore pulled back or in a giant three-strand braid, it never robbed her of her sense of humor. Or her passion for those who were on the outskirts of life. Or her unfaltering love for and devotion to her children — and especially her love for Blondie, who was the only man she ever loved and the only friend she ever needed.

The neighborhood began to change, too. The other neighborhood kids who had been so much a part of his Christmas Eve for so many years were, like his children, scattered across the country. His friends began to die or retire to Florida, where the warm breath of the Atlantic soothed the pain of arthritis and loneliness and reality.

For the first few years after Ellen died, his children and their families made an attempt to come home for Christmas. But they were never all there at the same time, and they stopped coming after a few years. He, too, made some efforts to visit them, but he always felt a little out of place. And it wasn't Christmas Eve unless it was on Deery Street.

Blondie was sitting in his easy chair next to the fireplace, looking at the pictures of all the grandchildren, twenty-three of them, crammed next to each other on the oak mantel. Above the fireplace was a wreath woven with red and green plaid ribbons and adorned with three gold stars that hung from the bottom. Ellen and the girls had made it the first Christmas after Ruth was born. A string of Christmas cards hung from one corner of the mantel to the other. He stopped putting up the floor-to-ceiling tree the year after Ellen died. He still had a tree because it wouldn't be Christmas without one, but it couldn't be very tall, though; the arthritis in his shoulders kept him from raising his arms high enough to put the star on the top.

Just as the grandfather clock in the hallway, which was always seven minutes fast, struck six times, he heard what he thought was a faint, small knock at the front door. He looked out the small, rectangular window in the top of the door, but didn't see anyone. The knock sounded again. Opening the door, he saw two small children. They couldn't have been more than four or five. They stepped back as he opened the screen door.

"Are you Blondie?" the boy asked.

They were fraternal twins. He held her hand. She clutched a small package wrapped in bright red paper, with white ribbon around the corners.

"Yes, I'm Blondie," he responded as he stooped down so he could see their faces. "And who might you be?"

"I'm Blondie, too. But that's not my real name. My real name is Othello Lafayette. But everyone just calls me Blondie. This is my sister, Ellen Colleen, but she just goes by Ellen."

Blondie fell back, catching himself with both hands, and sat in the doorway. He was speechless. All the years rushed before him as he watched the light from the Christmas tree dance in their eyes.

Ellen stuck out her hand with the small package. "You're supposed to open this now. It's your Christmas present from our daddy."

He took the present and began to unwrap it. Every seam had three or four layers of tape. They had obviously wrapped it. It was a five by seven picture frame. As he sat there looking at the picture, his heart raced. He could hardly breathe. It was a black and white picture of him and Ellen sitting on the front wall. Her mother had taken it the day they moved in across the street. It had disappeared more years ago than he could remember. It was his favorite picture. Always would be.

"Blondie?" It was a familiar voice.

Blondie looked up. Around the corner of the porch stood Roger. The twins ran to him, each putting their arms around one of his legs.

"When I left for the army, I took the picture. You and Ellen took me in when no one else wanted me. You made me a part of your family. You were the only real parents I ever knew. I took the picture because it was the only one of both of you together. I've kept it with me always. It has been with me all over the world. And every night I've given thanks that Frank found me sitting on the wall and brought me here on Christmas Eve. I've been too ashamed to give it back. I know how you loved her and how much you loved that picture.

"I'm worth a lot of money. And I owe it all, everything I've done that's good in my life, to you and Ellen and Frank and the girls. I have no excuses for losing touch. When I learned that Ellen had died, I wanted to come but I couldn't bear to see you heartbroken. Then I learned that Christmas Eve on Deery Street had ceased. So, I'm here with my family to try and make tonight like it used to be."

Blondie was speechless. Big tears streamed down his face.

"Okay, kids. You know what to do."

They each took one of his hands, helped him up, and led him to the front railing. While he was listening to Roger, he hadn't noticed that a crowd had gathered on the sidewalk in front of the house. Roger pulled a small flashlight from his pocket and turned it on. Instantly, the sidewalk and street were filled with what seemed to be hundreds of tiny lights that flickered up and down Deery Street from end to end. There were friends and neighbors he hadn't seen in years. There were children and grandchildren and great-grandchildren of friends and neighbors.

Standing in front were all seven of his children. There was Magdalene and Jake, who was now a member of Congress. He still rode a Harley and he still smoked Lucky Strikes. And he did have a tattoo of a heart with "Magdalene" written in the center. While Ellen had been his greatest critic, she also became his greatest supporter. When he first ran for Congress she raised over ten thousand dollars in donations, each no more than a hundred dollars. Most were twenty-five. When she died, Jake had

15

sobbed uncontrollably.

Frank stood next to Roger's wife. Sarah, the serial marrier, was with husband number five. In front of them, standing on the wall that had been such an important part of life on Deery Street, were all twenty-three of his grandchildren.

"Roger, how did this happen? Why?"

"I told you; I'm worth a lot of money. But the 'how' isn't important. The 'why' is."

Roger stepped to the front of the railing and lifted the twins up, so they were standing on the railing in front of Blondie.

"Blondie wants to know why you all are here."

In unison, they all roared, "Because everyone has to have a place to go on Christmas."

NANNY'S LOCKET

NANNY'S LOCKET

She stood looking at everything but looking at nothing. Just remembering. The front porch was the home for the metal glider that creaked and groaned like the rusted hinges of a wooden gate, the product of years of rain and children trying to see how hard they could push with their little feet which just barely touched the wooden slats of the porch. The two oldest grandchildren, in a fierce display of summer boredom, actually did turn it over, resulting in six stitches across one's left eyebrow, and one less tooth for the other. That glider had heard more stories and lies, especially when her husband recounted all the giant fish he caught and the whales that got away, than she could ever remember. The street had seen the world change from trolleys that clicked and clacked and sparked on their journeys, connecting families and neighborhoods and the town, to cars with nearly every modern convenience which practically drove themselves, and filled the air with rumbles and fumes that made her cough if she sat on the porch too long.

She had stood in front of this particular window on Christmas Eve for many, many years. It was an annual vigil. Her reminiscing soothed the passing time, restored her spirit, and still gave her a sense of awe for all she had seen and heard and done.

For many years she always wore the same thing on Christmas Eve: a red, narrow-wale corduroy jumper that fell almost to her ankles. It was plain yet purposeful, simple but elegant, at least as much as a corduroy jumper could be. She wore a bright white blouse underneath. It was starched and crisply ironed, and looked like it came straight from the laundry. Of course, she would never send clothes to the laundry. That would be "uppity." She always told her daughters and her daughters' daughters, "True elegance is alluring, yet understated." Her fashion philosophy was stretched to its limit by the daughters that went to college in the sixties. Tie-dyed shirts and bell-bottomed pants were not permitted through the front door. The neighbors would surely think that her girls had become nothing but trash. How would she be able to face the women at the WCTU? Only reluctantly did she allow them to sneak in through the back door. It seemed better than having them strip down to their underwear in the backyard. Given the moral decadence of the youth of that era, she was always afraid that they wouldn't have on any underwear, and that they would strip naked just to exert their newfound independence.

The only jewelry she wore with the Christmas jumper was her wedding band and a small, silver-plated, heart-shaped locket that was inscribed "To Joy, Love Bill." It was the first thing her husband had given her some fifty-two years ago when they were first courting. She wore it always. Her mother thought it was a cheap, tawdry trinket. But then her mother was more impressed with style than substance. It was her most prized possession. A few years ago, the locket — along with other personal items that had no value to anyone but her — was stolen by some neighborhood thugs. She had felt naked without it.

It was more than just a locket. It symbolized almost fifty years of living and loving. The locket had seen her husband through three wars. It had seen poverty and personal triumph. It had birthed babies and buried friends. It was all her hopes and dreams. It contained all that she had been, and was.

She felt a tug on both sides of her jumper, which quickly became a back and forth contest to see who could pull the fastest.

"Children, stop pulling on Nanny's dress. You'll stretch it all out of shape. What is it you want, anyway?" She continued to look out of the window, her breath creating clouds on it as she spoke. She smiled as she remembered all of the times she had cleaned fingerprint faces and messages about her children's undying love and devotion to whomever was their love du jour.

"Pop's gonna tell us a story. We want you to come sit with us."

"I don't know if I'm up to a story tonight."

"He hasn't told us a story in a really, really, really long time. Please come sit with us. Please. Please. Please!"

Their supplication was too much.

"All right, I'll come. But you have to help me keep him on the story."

The adult women were in the kitchen, washing and drying the good china and silver. The men still sat at the dining room table, drinking coffee from handmade mugs that had been in the family for longer than anyone could remember. No one actually knew who had made them or where they had come from. They were easily four or five hundred years old; that's certainly what they had been led to believe. The men were usually very good to help with the dishes. However, they were absolutely forbidden to handle the good stuff. They were lucky to even use the good stuff. It was one of Nanny's hard and fast, set in stone, without equivocation rules: at no time is a man to do anything with the good china and silver. It had always been a rule. It was not a gender issue; it was a clumsiness issue.

The teenage grandchildren were seated, reluctantly, on the living room divan, their arms folded across their chests.

Their body language clearly indicated they were totally bored, as if to say, "Another of Pop's stories. I wonder how many times we've heard this one. Oh, boy! I can hardly wait!"

The pre-pubescent kids had taken the green felt table pads off the dining room table and, along with several patchwork quilts (ones that truly were family heirlooms), had made a pallet on the living room floor. They were very adept at making pallets; these were what they slept on when they came and spent the night.

They would lie on their stomachs with their chins on their arms, which were folded on top of old, clumpy down pillows. They would lie like that for hours, talking of fame and fortune, love lost and love found. The world was simple and understandable and glorious. It was a ritual reserved for only those who were worthy of the pallet. As the kids outgrew this nocturnal tradition, the vacancies could be filled only by those who had proven themselves. Permission had to be given by the one vacating his or her spot. Pallet positions were deadly serious, with equally deadly consequences.

Nanny would never forget the time she was awakened in the middle of the night by the screams of one of the younger children. Without even putting on her robe, which clearly indicated that someone was at death's door, she ran to the bathroom from whence the torturous screams were coming. She flung open the door and found the two oldest boys holding one of the younger boys upside-down by his ankles above the toilet. His nightshirt was down over his arms and head. Part of it was on the seat, and part was in the toilet. It seemed this young interloper had snuck into the pallet when no vacancy had been declared. They were simply teaching him the importance of the pallet position progression.

All the grandkids had taken their places. Nanny was sitting in her wingback chair located next to the front door, very close to where she had been standing earlier. Pop's chair was a cane-bottom, ladder-back chair, the one that went with the cherry secretary that stood in the corner perpendicular to the front window. He would sit there for hours, working crossword puzzles or filling out entry forms for every mail-order contest he could find. He'd never won anything, but he was convinced he would. Win enough money to retire to Florida and fish.

"Tell us our favorite story, Pop. Please?" came the request from the younger and middle groups. The older group just sat on the couch, not believing that they had allowed themselves to be talked into hearing Pop's worn-out stories one more time.

"Hold the phone," he said, an expression he used a lot. "I can't tell all the favorite stories tonight."

Each group had a favorite, but everyone liked the one about how he had lost his eye in a hunting accident as a boy. Midway through the story, he would take out his glass eye and roll it around in his mouth, swishing it from cheek to cheek. One time, he had gotten choked and spit out the eye, which promptly rolled across the floor and down the furnace grate. Fortunately, it had been stuck just under the grate. However, the impact of the eye hitting the floor after being jettisoned from his mouth had cracked it straight across the middle, which created the illusion that he actually had two eyes in one socket. The kids loved that. Needless to say, that was the last time he did the eye-in-the-mouth trick.

"I want to tell you a story I've never told you before."

A new story? Could this be? Really, a new story? The idea of a new story sparked everyone's interest, even the delinquents on the divan.

Pop was smaller than average. His hair was salt and pepper, but hadn't thinned much at all. He wore octagonal shaped wire-rimmed glasses, ones he had had for years. The prescription had been changed several times, but not the frames. He had permanent dark circles under his eyes from years and years of working two and three jobs so that his children could go to college. He was not formally educated himself, but he and Nanny had insisted that their children would be college-educated — and they all were.

He was extremely intelligent, well read, and articulate. He loved to read, and he read anything. He never passed up a chance to engage in thoughtful discussions about any topic. He was always the champion of the downtrodden, at least as much as their resources would allow. He was not very emotional, except when moved to extremes. He dearly loved his children and his grandchildren.

Everything had gotten quiet. Even the adults were seated quietly around the dining room table. The word of a new story had spread throughout the house.

"It was Christmas, 1943. Times were hard. Even though the Depression was officially over, everyone around here still felt the effects. The war was raging in Europe and in the Pacific. Everyone hoped that the war would be over soon. And I was afraid, because I knew if it wasn't over soon I would join the army when I graduated from high school — something some of you ought to consider — and would be sent off to fight.

"I was sixteen and I had my first girlfriend. She was the prettiest girl in school, and I couldn't believe she liked me, too. The first time I saw her was the winter before. She was getting out of a big, black car with a shiny silver ornament on the hood, in front of the school. It had snowed the night before. We had to go to school when it snowed. You don't know how good you've got it. She started walking down the walkway toward some other girls, who waited for her to catch up. For some reason she stopped, turned and looked in my direction. I thought I was going to die. I dropped my books on purpose so I wouldn't have to look at her. Of course, the snow didn't help my homework any. I'm sure she thought I was a complete buffoon, and I was sure she and her friends were talking about my lack of co-ordination. As I watched her, she looked like an angel walking in the snow. I fell desperately in love with her from that instant."

"Who was she?"

"Did she fall in love with you, too?"

"What was her name?"

Excited questions rang out from the group.

"Her name was Joy."

"That's Nanny's name," someone said.

"That's right. It was your grandmother."

Everyone had moved closer; the adults, the middle kids. The delinquents were still on the divan, but they were leaning forward, elbows on their knees, so they could hear.

"Get back to the story, Pop," came from one of his children.

"I carried newspapers in the mornings before school, and I bagged groceries after school. Whatever money I needed, I had to earn myself. I had saved and saved so I could buy your grandmother something special for our first Christmas. I searched this town over for just the right gift. But everything I really liked was too expensive. Everything I could afford was cheap and tacky. I didn't know what I was going to do. Time was running out. Then I found it: the perfect gift."

"What was it? What was it?"

"It was a silver, heart-shaped locket with a silver necklace."

"You mean like the one Nanny used to wear?"

"It was the same one."

"The same one?"

"The very same one. Even though I had been in love with her for almost a year, we hadn't been dating for that long. Her present was to be a surprise. When I finally found what I wanted, it was two days before Christmas. Because I had to carry papers and work at the grocery store on Christmas Eve, I knew I wouldn't have much time to get it to her. And to make things worse, it snowed eight inches on Christmas Eve morning. I figured that my only course of action was to take the present by her house after I finished carrying my papers on Christmas morning. I knew that I might not be able to give it to her myself, but at least she would have it on Christmas. Christmas morning, I hurried as fast as I could to finish my paper route. I wanted to give her present first thing, or at least have it there when she woke up."

"Gee, Pop, I didn't know you were so romantic," his least favorite son-in-law commented sarcastically.

This son-in-law was twenty-five going on fifteen. He was from a rich family in Boston; a pseudo-aristocrat. He wanted to go to an Ivy League school, but his daddy had gone to one of the best schools in the South on an athletic scholarship. He had also graduated with honors. So, as fathers will do sometimes, he insisted that his son go to his alma mater. His son had no scholarship, just his daddy's name and money. Pop's daughter met him in college. She was on a full academic scholarship; something Pop never let him forget.

With a look that would stare-down Satan himself, Pop fired back, "There's a lot about me you don't know, young man. There's a lot you don't know, period." He said it with a grin. Some weren't sure if he was kidding. Those

25

that needed to know he was serious knew it.

"As I said, it had snowed the day before — about eight or nine, maybe ten, inches. The wind was blowing hard, so hard that I just couldn't roll the newspapers and throw them on the porches as I normally did. I had to put them behind the screen doors to keep them from blowing off."

"Pop, are you sure it was only ten inches and not ten feet? And were you still barefooted because you couldn't afford shoes, like when you had to walk to school every day in ten feet of snow for fifteen miles, with only a piece of bread and four crackers for lunch?" questioned one of the divan delinquents, but in a lighthearted way.

"Aw-right, smart guy," he said with a grin. "You'd have never made it in my day. Do you want to hear this story or not?

"It was bitter cold, about fifteen degrees. The wind swayed the leafless trees back and forth in a wistful wonderland ballet. The temperature had warmed just enough the day before to melt the snow on the sidewalks, which re-froze Christmas Eve night. In fact, I fell several times carrying papers that morning. And each time, I fell squarely on my rear end. The seat of my pants had a wet spot that perfectly outlined each cheek. My nose was red and running. My eyes watered, the tears immediately freezing as they ran down my cheeks. I looked like an icicle with eyes. It took me about an hour to walk the two miles to your grandmother's house.

"She lived in a deceptively small house. It was fairly long across the front, but it wasn't very deep. In those days, houses were built very close together. As I'd walk by, many times going out of my way hoping to catch a glimpse of her, it looked really big from the front. But in fact, it wasn't any bigger than my house, which wasn't big at all.

"After trudging through the waist-deep snow," he said, pausing to look at his captivated audience and chuckling out loud at his clever exaggeration, "and ice and wind, feeling much like a postman, I finally got there. I noticed that the Christmas tree was the only thing lit in the house. The blue and green and red lights shown brightly through the window. The light from a nearby street lamp made the tinsel and icicles sparkle like the stars just after the sun sets and the moon rises, the time when only they light up the sky. The sun was just below the horizon, casting a blue-gray blanket across the world. It was that time each day when we were still innocent, when life was simple, when fairy dust still sparkled on the eyelids of sleeping children.

"As I crossed the street, I noticed someone sweeping the steps and porch of her house. I thought it was weird because the snow had already been cleared. It was a woman whose back was to me. She had just bent down to pick something up, so all I could see was from her butt down."

"How'd you know it was a woman, then?" The least favorite son-in-law never passed up a chance to get in a dig.

"Well, since she had on a flowered housecoat and had lace around the bottoms of her pajamas, I figured it was either a woman or a really sweet man. I assumed the former. Any more questions, son?"

Silence.

"Since she hadn't heard me approach, I stood at the bottom of the steps, not wanting to startle her, and said, 'Excuse me, ma'am.'

"I startled her anyway. I'm sure she didn't expect anyone to be at the bottom of the steps at that early hour. She stood straight up, spinning around as she did. And as she did, she slipped on the slick porch and fell. There she sat, her knees bent to about eye-level. Her hair was rolled with objects I'd never seen before, and still haven't. She had a bandanna that covered her ears, came up around the sides of her face, and was tied in a knot just above her forehead. She looked like Rosie the Riveter in all those 'support the war' posters. She was desperately trying to cover her night clothes with her robe, which had come untied when she fell, but her hair never moved.

"She rolled over onto her knees as ladylike as she could and reached for the railing. But the banister wasn't as close as she thought. This time she ended up on her face, spread-eagled on the porch. I hurried up the steps to try and help. Forgetting that the steps were slick, I tried skipping every other step. However, I caught the toe of my foot on the top step, and I fell too. You guessed it; I fell on her just as she was getting to her knees again. We both went down on the porch with a very loud *oomph*. And there we were: her lying face-down, me lying on top of her. We were like two spoons lying there on the front porch in fifteen degree weather. And her hair still hadn't moved.

"We lay there perfectly motionless. I thought she was dead. I wanted to be. Then she said calmly, matter-of-factly, 'Young man, please remove yourself from off of me. And do so very, very slowly.' I did as I was told — something some of you should practice more often — and slowly eased myself off her. Once I was standing, I tried to help her. Of course, after my display of grace and coordination, she would have none of that. She stood, straightened her robe, and then turned around and looked me straight in the eyes.

"'Whom might you be, young man?'

"'I'm Bill.'

"'Bill who?'

"'I'm Bill. My daddy calls me Billy.' I couldn't remember my last name. I couldn't remember anything other than 'I'm Bill.'

"'Are you the young man that is trying to court Miss Joy?'

"I did manage to get out 'yes, ma'am' and not 'I'm Bill' again.

"'And what, may I ask, are you doing here at this hour?'

"I was frozen. I stood there expecting to have her broom rammed down my throat.

"'I brought Joy's, I mean Miss Joy's Christmas present. I was just going to leave it behind the door.' Which really wasn't true; I was going to knock on the door and ask to see her. But I wasn't about to say that.

"'Young man, young ladies do not receive gentleman callers at this hour. And they certainly don't receive them unannounced.'

"I was shivering more from fear than from cold.

"'If you would like to come back at two o'clock this afternoon, I'm sure she would see you then.'

"'Two o'clock. Yes, ma'am. Yes ma'am, two o'clock.' I turned – carefully this time – and got away as fast as I could.

"On the way home, I tried to figure out who this woman was. The best I could determine was that she must have been the maid. It made sense that Joy's family would have a maid. She rode to school sometimes in a big, black limousine-looking car. She lived in a big house. The woman had referred to her as 'Miss Joy.' And no one except a maid would be out sweeping the porch and steps that didn't need sweeping. Must be nice to have someone do your chores.

"At fifteen before two, I stood at the bottom of those same steps. Coat and tie, dress pants – I had a blue pair and a brown pair – hair slicked back with a little dab of Brylcream. The temperature had warmed up some, but it was

29

still very cold. Given that morning's interlude with the maid, I wanted to ring the doorbell at exactly two o'clock. So, I stood at the bottom of the steps, freezing my buns off, for an extra fifteen minutes.

"At exactly two o'clock I rang the doorbell, and the door was promptly opened by the other spoon. What a difference a few hours can make. This was not the same woman that had been face-down on the porch. Rosie the Riveter should look this good. She had on a flowing, empire-waist, crimson dress. She wore pearl earrings and a pearl necklace that hung about six inches from the top of the dress. I later learned that the pearls were fake – good fakes, but fake nevertheless. Her nails were nicely manicured. She had classic facial features. And the radio transistors were gone from her hair.

"'My name is Bill. May I please see Joy, I mean Miss Joy?' I don't know what it was, but I don't think that I ever did tell her my last name. The trauma of lying on top of an older woman must have been too great for my adolescent psyche.

"'Yes, young man, I know you're Bill. Won't you please come in? I'll see if Miss Joy can see you now.' She proceeded to go about halfway up the stairs inside. 'Miss Joy, a young gentleman is here to see you.' Then she started back down the steps toward me.

"'Oh, no! I thought to myself, 'I'll have to talk to her. I can't tell her my whole name. How am I going to have a conversation?' By this time, I had taken the present out of my overcoat pocket and was holding it with both hands in front of me.

"My front porch partner was now standing in front of me. I could hear footsteps above me, approaching the stairs. Not wanting this woman to think that all I could say was 'I'm Bill,' I blurted out the first thing that came to mind.

"'What's it like being a maid? Do you make pretty good money? I'm sure more than carrying papers and bagging groceries. Don't you get Christmas off? It doesn't seem fair to have to work on Christmas.'

"She just stood there, with her mouth open, glaring at me like she wanted to hang me by my bow tie – which had taken me one hour to tie so it would be perfect, and which my mom had had to finish tying for me.

"By this time, Joy had appeared. 'Merry Christmas, Bill. I see you've already met Mother.'

"'Mother?'

"'Yes, young man. Mother, not maid. Mother.'

"I looked at the woman, then looked back at Joy. Then back at the woman.

"'Mother?' World War Two was no longer a threat. I was going to die right there in the foyer of their house. I was speechless. I couldn't even say, 'I'm Bill.' Then I began speaking in tongues, dropped the present, ran out the front door, slipped and fell in about the same spot as before, and bounced down the steps and out into the street, which was now slushy from melting snow. I ran all the way home just mumbling, 'Mother. Mother. Mother.'

"And that's the story of how Nanny got her locket."

Everyone looked at Nanny, who was grinning from ear to ear.

"What happened? Obviously, you overcame Pop's major faux pas." This came, rather sincerely, from the least favorite son-in-law.

"He avoided me for weeks. It was like he fell off the earth."

"I was humiliated. I couldn't bear to see her."

"One time at school, he even ducked into the girl's restroom when he saw me coming down the hall."

"So, what happened?" asked one of the kids.

"I waited for him after his last class one day, literally pushed him against his locker and held him there with one hand, and shook my finger at him."

"What did you say?"

"Did you yell at him?"

"Did you smack him?"

"What I said was, 'Bill Roberts, quit acting stupid! I can't believe you've been avoiding me. But I don't care about what happened.' I had the locket around my neck. I held it up right in his face. 'This is the most wonderful present I've ever received. I'll wear it always. Do you want me to be your girl, or not?'"

"What did he say?" the least favorite son-in-law asked.

Pop reached in his coat pocket and pulled out a small, brightly wrapped package. He looked at everyone. "I said," he began, then looked at Nanny, "'Will you be my girl?'" Pop handed her the gift. Nanny sat there. She seemed afraid to open it.

Everyone, including the least favorite son-in-law, began saying, "Open it! We want to see what it is! Hurry! Open it!"

She began pulling the taped edges away from the paper until it came away from the small box inside, then lifted the lid. Tears began to stream down her face as she took out a silver necklace with a silver locket. The locket read, "To Joy, Love Bill." It was her locket. The house suddenly became perfectly still, perfectly silent.

Pop spoke. "Last month when I was raking leaves, I thought I noticed something shining in the grass. So I raked harder, and this is what I found. Apparently, the thugs dropped it and then stepped on it, burying it in the soft, wet soil. So I took it and had it cleaned up."

He then took the locket from her hand, placed it around her neck, and kissed her.

***

Everyone had gone. The house was quiet. No more sounds of radio-controlled cars running into table legs, or people legs. She was again standing before of the front window, gently rubbing the locket between her thumb and index finger, as she had done for so many years. She didn't notice that Pop had come to stand behind her. He bent over her shoulder and blew his breath on the window, making a big cloud on the glass. He took her hand, closing all her fingers except one. And with both of their fingers he wrote, "To Joy, Love Bill."

MAGIC SOCKS

MAGIC SOCKS

"Are you awake?" came the small, half-whimpering voice; a sound that usually meant he was about to become wise man, arbiter or executioner in the very near future.

He rolled over toward the outside of the bed and opened one eye, still unsure if the voice that had interrupted the solemnity of his solitary slumber was real or some untimely aberration. Just as he thought: Katie, the youngest of his five children, was squarely eyeball-to-eyeball.

He had been blessed with two sets of twins. Maggie and Mona were high school seniors. They were usually referred to simply as "the girls." They were bright, funny, and strikingly beautiful — a deadly combination. Everyone, especially boys, wanted to be around them.

Jeff and Josh were typical fourteen-year-olds, lost somewhere between the man-child and the child-man. He usually referred to them as "the boys." The girls always referred to them much more descriptively. They were legends at the arcade, but couldn't do the simplest tasks around the house without breaking something. They liked girls and talked about them all the time. But when they talked with girls, they spoke some strange language only Swahili witchdoctors could understand. Everything was confusing and uncertain in their lives. But there was one thing about which they were certain: their father had an IQ of twelve. And since he'd been around since dirt, it was obvious that he understood nothing about being a teenage boy.

"What's the matter, sweetheart? What time is it anyway?" Things were too quiet for it to be very late.

"It's early."

"How early?"

"It's pretty early."

"Exactly, how pretty early is it?"

"Exactly?"

"Yes, exactly!" He looked at the clock. "Why are you crying at forty-two minutes after five on Saturday morning? And why are you doing it in my bedroom?" He didn't mean to sound insensitive, but sleep — restful sleep, anyway — was something that didn't happen often. And when it did, it was usually between four o'clock and seven o'clock on Saturday mornings.

He wriggled out from under the covers and propped himself up against the headboard, raising his arm. As if on cue, she snuggled in beside him, one arm around his back and the other around his stomach. He began stroking silky strand after silky strand of her coal-black hair, removing the tangles from the night's sleep.

He thought of all the nights he had done the same thing after his wife died. All the times Katie had awakened in the middle of the night. How she had found safety there, and how he found safety with her there. They knew the routine by heart.

"I'm not really upset-crying. I'm mad-crying!"

"Mad about what?"

"I can't find my magic Christmas socks. I bet those dumb boys hid them on purpose. They'd do that, you know."

Originally, the socks were red with white, frilly lace around the tops. They had "The Littlest Angel" on the outside of each ankle. They were Christmas socks like all Christmas socks found in any Wal-Mart. In fact, that's where they'd been bought. They hadn't cost much, but then most magical things don't.

Now, the socks only vaguely resembled what they used to look like. One angel had come off in the wash; the other was barely hanging on by her halo. Neither sock was red; rather a dull pink, with occasional beige spots, the result of unexpectedly being bleached. A sin for which he had only recently been forgiven. They were too small, barely coming to her ankles. Her middle right toe was beginning to protrude through the seam, and the left heel was half gone. But she wouldn't part with them. She wore them on every special occasion — Christmas, Easter, the Fourth of July. It didn't matter. After all, they were her special magic socks.

"Now, sweetie, I don't think the boys would do that. And besides, you can't jump to that conclusion like that."

"Sure I can!"

She was right. They would do something like that.

"I've gotta find my socks. I've just gotta!" Tears began to flow rather freely.

"I know the socks are special. And we'll find them. But why are they so important right now, especially at fifty-six minutes after five in the morning?"

"If I don't find my socks, I'll forget my lines in the Christmas play tonight. Or my halo will fall off. Or something else awful will happen. And everybody will laugh at me. I'm the most important angel, you know."

He understood the magic in special socks. He had a pair in little league; the pair he had on when he hit his first home run. It was one of his defining moments. He refused to wear any others from then on. And he absolutely refused to let his mother wash them. The magic was in the red clay rings around the ankles. He was convinced of two things: The bigger the rings, the better he would play; and if his mom washed them, the magic would be gone. He would be forever doomed to baseball oblivion and anonymity. Never to hit the World-series-winning homer for the Yankees in the bottom of the ninth. Never to be "The Mick's" successor, or hear him say, "Nice catch, kid."

It became quite a challenge to keep his mom, Mrs. "be sure you have on clean underwear and socks whenever you go anyplace," from exorcizing the red clay magic he had worked so hard to gain. Most mothers only required clean underwear. His threw in clean socks. He never understood why. Probably some misguided concept about personal hygiene. She obviously knew nothing about the finer nuances of athletic prowess.

***

The past few Christmases had been halfhearted. His wife's death left him unprepared and unaccustomed to being both father and mother, something fate or God had viciously and surprisingly inflicted on his ordered, predictable life.

They had not been in their own home at Christmas since her death. Both sets of grandparents welcomed the opportunity for them to visit at Christmas. He rationalized that both their parents shouldn't really be traveling, and it gave the kids a chance to spend time with their grandparents. But more than anything, he could deflect the pain and avoid the fear that he couldn't make Christmas like it had always been. He would rather endure the hassles of getting everything done early, packing, and driving six hours because at Grammy's house, everything would get done. Nothing would be screwed-up or left out. He was safe there.

The first trip taught him valuable lessons. Women who listen to classical music during pregnancy have children with very tiny bladders. That must be true, because every time he played one of his favorite classical selections, someone had to go to the bathroom. He also learned that four out of five dentists recommend that people over forty should not listen to Toad the Wet Sprocket. It had something to do with extreme teeth grinding. He had questions about the fifth dentist. Probably too much nitrous oxide.

For the kids, the novelty of a grandparents' Christmas wore off quickly. He understood their frustration and disappointment. They were away from their friends. The older girls had boyfriends who had apparently moved into his house like thieves in the night, an appropriate term given the quadrupled grocery bills. Compared to previous loves, these boys actually weren't too bad. They had some manners, except at the table. They called him sir. He liked that. They could occasionally speak in multi-syllabic terms. They adored his girls — something he wasn't thrilled with. And they had exquisite taste in earrings. The boys didn't like being with anyone except other fourteen-year-old boys.

"Daddy," Katie said, her voice smaller now. "Will you help me find my socks?"

"Sure I will. Let me clean up a little. We'll look for them after breakfast. Is that okay?"

She nodded her approval of their reconnaissance. "I'm gonna go look in the boys' room."

"Don't go in there right now. You'll wake them up."

"So? They'd do it to me."

"That's not the point. Just because they're inconsiderate doesn't make it right, or that that's the way you should be. Besides, I don't want you going in there alone. It's too dangerous for anyone going in there without an armed guard. Why don't you search your room again? You know, sometimes we look for things so hard and so long, and we want them so badly, that we look right over them

— when they've been right in front of us the whole time."

"Okay, I'll look again." Which was accompanied by a this-is-a-waste-of-time-but-I'll-do-it-to-make-you-happy look.

Striding determinedly through the translucent half-light in his bedroom, off she went. A woman with a mission, mumbling, "I'll find the socks or I'll kill the boys."

The kids were at the ages when they were gone all the time. The girls were eighteen and basically had their own lives. He mostly provided cash, car keys, and a place for cheap dates. He wasn't sure what the boys did. He just knew he had to take them a lot of places or they could never achieve their "ultimate level of coolty." Saturday mornings were the exception — they had breakfast together. It was sacred. Ah yes, how everyone had grown to love these times of family festivities and fun, these moments of concern and compassion, these times of endearment and enjoyment that came when his children gathered, gratefully seeking the knowledge and wisdom imparted by father-dear at the kitchen table.

One particular Saturday morning, he sat half-dazed at the kitchen table. Not from the remains of family breakfast that seemed to cover every inch of counter space, but from being overwhelmed. Too much had happened. Too little time. Too much to do. Too little energy. He had never truly done Christmas. Never cooked the whole meal. Never helped everyone with their shopping. Or all of the decorating. Or whole-house cleaning. Or addressed the Christmas cards. He'd done some of everything, but never all of it at once. He had mostly observed and enjoyed. And this year he had to help Katie get ready for the annual Christmas pageant.

The faint trills of a distant angel snatched him from his holiday self-pity. He traced the source to the smallest, though still roomy, of the four bedrooms. Katie's room. She was searching slowly but meticulously through a pile of dolls and clothes, both hers and the dolls'. It was obvious the magic socks had not been uncovered.

She was singing the theme song from her favorite movie, one the two of them had seen together. He liked the song when he first heard it. When she sang it in the car on the way home, it became his favorite.

Katie had perfect pitch and an extraordinarily gifted voice, one any adult would be proud to have. It could be big or small, powerful or disarmingly therapeutic. It was very strange to hear such a mature, polished voice coming from such a small girl. Folks came from all over to hear her sing. Each note was as clear as the sounds from the creek that rushed past a friend's mountain cabin on its way from the near-by mountains that touched the sky. The place where they spent their mid-August vacations.

"Hi, sweetie."

"I still haven't found my magic socks."

"Where have you looked?"

"I've looked everywhere. I really don't think the boys took them. They're not that stupid. They know how important they are to me. Any they know you'd kill them real bad. I'm scared I won't find them."

He sat down in front of her, his legs crossed Indian-style, just as she was sitting. They were separated only by the array of ten-year-old paraphernalia piled in the middle of the floor. He took both of her tiny hands in his.

"You know, Katie, I had a pair of magic socks once. I wore them to play baseball. I always wore them. I used to hide them from Grammy so she wouldn't wash them."

"Didn't they stink real bad?"

"As a matter of fact, they did. But I didn't care. They had dirty brown rings around the ankles. That was where the magic was. If Grammy washed them, then all the magic would be gone, and I wouldn't be able to play anymore. Or at least that's what I thought."

"Did you play in them forever?"

"Let me ask you a question. What socks did I have on last summer when I played ball?"

"I guess you had on the socks Maggie and Mona gave you for Father's Day one year. You know, the ugly ones that fall down around your ankles."

"That's right. So I didn't have on my magic socks, then, did I?"

"No, I don't guess you did."

"How'd I play?"

"Okay, I guess. But I don't really remember. The boys kept pouring dirt down my underwear."

"Since you don't remember, I played really well. And I did it without my magic socks."

"That's different."

"How's it different?"

"I don't know. It just is." She was about to cry, afraid she was right and it was different.

"Katie, there's a lot of magic in the world. It's everywhere. But it's not in socks, sweetie. It's in people. It's down deep inside. In our hearts. It's in the dreams you think about when you lay in the grass in the summertime and trace the Big Dipper with your finger. It's in all of us. When you sing, it's magical. Your voice makes an invisible cloud that surrounds everyone that hears you, and we feel warm and wonderful inside."

He knew she was afraid to believe him. She had always had her socks.

"I'll forget my part. Or I'll sing bad notes."

"You'll be great! But if you do forget your lines, then just tell us your part in your own words. You know the story of Baby Jesus by heart. There are no right words, only right meanings. We'll keep looking for the socks. Just remember, Katie, the magic's in you, not the socks. And no matter what, I'm proud of you and I love you.

**

The church sanctuary was filled with parents and grandparents and all manner of relatives and friends, each adorned with some form of photographic equipment. Others were there just to hear her. The church was a fairly small neighborhood church. Special events were really big deals.

Katie was one of those that thought she was late if she wasn't an hour early. Because she was the most important angel, they were at the church before anyone, including the custodian. She said it was so she could get her "mental mind" properly prepared for a performance that would make the Baby Jesus happy. He knew better. The socks had not been found. She was hoping for some kind of divine intercession. This was, after all, the season of miracles.

He had forced the boys to come, but had agreed to let them sit with two fourteen-year-old girls and their parents. It was most definitely uncool to sit with him. While it was uncool to be sitting with anyone's parents, anywhere, sitting next to the prettiest girls in their class more than compensated for their parents being there too. All the other boys would clearly see how studly they were.

The older twins had dates. Their plans didn't include the Christmas pageant. "I'll save four seats, just in case," he had said, which brought a "Get real," in two-part harmony.

He was seated where Katie had requested — stage left, four rows back, an aisle seat. She had to be able to find him, especially since she didn't have on her magic socks. In fact, she had on no socks. She was taking no chances.

"Sir? Are these seats taken?" It was a familiar but out of place voice.

"I was saving these, but I guess they're not com...."

It was the girls. His girls. With their boyfriends, who looked none too happy, firmly in tow.

Mona bent over and whispered, "Scoot over. We want to sit with you." When they were younger, they always demanded that he sit between them. His wife had had to sit between the boys. She was more graceful at stepping over people when the boys had to be escorted out during performances. She hadn't seen the end of many things.

"I thought you had other plans?"

"We did," Maggie proclaimed, "We decided we wanted to come. You're not the only one who loves to hear Katie sing, you know."

"The goons don't look very happy." He called all their boyfriends goons. The girls were offended by the term at first. But they had grown to recognize that boyfriends symbolized that one day, some man would take them away. And he would be left, again.

"We gave them the choice: Go to the pageant and be with us, or don't go to the pageant and don't be with us. Ta-da!"

They both leaned close. "It's great having power over men, Dad!" they said, with supreme confidence.

He leaned forward and glared, then grinned at their wimpy little boyfriends. *And you thought you could replace me. Ha! Guess I showed you. Thought you could horn in on my territory, did ya? Think again, dudes!* he thought to himself.

***

45

It was just about time for the big scene; the one where the most important angel was to proclaim to the shepherds the arrival of the Christ child.

A small group of shepherds clad in bright, vertical-striped bathrobes, towels of corresponding colors tied around their foreheads, had gathered at one side of the stage. They rubbed their arms and hands over the few logs constituting a fake fire to warm themselves. A multitude of stars — some with four points, others with five or six; some big, some little — hung all over the blue velvet curtains behind them. In the middle was one giant, glorious star that outshone the others. They paternally watched their flock of cotton-ball-covered cardboard sheep and talked quietly among themselves.

Then, there she was, walking toward the shepherds. But something was wrong. Her halo had slipped to the side of her head, and part of the garland hung down to her shoulders in a shiny, silver loop. She was unaware. They had made the halo out of a coat hanger that afternoon, a duty put off because it was something he had never done before. As usual, he avoided making it until he had no choice. And as usual, there wasn't enough time to do it properly.

With every step, the halo slipped a little more. She stopped mid-stage and faced the audience. The halo was barely on, much like the remaining angel on her magic socks. His heart was pounding. He wanted to run onto the stage and fix it.

"And there were in the same country, shepherds, abiding in the field, keeping watch over their flocks by night." She spoke clearly, confidently.

The halo had held its place so far.

Then the angel chorus proclaimed, "And lo, the angel of the Lord came upon them. And the glory of the Lord shown round about them. And they were so afraid. And the angel said unto them...."

She had moved in front of the shepherds. Gracefully, almost whimsically, she raised her arms as if to gather the flock.

"Fear not..." As she began to speak, the halo fell to the floor and rolled to the edge of the stage, well out of immediate reach. His heart sank. All the color instantly disappeared from her cheeks. A collective gasp ricocheted antiphonally throughout the church. Then silence. Tomb silence.

Katie stood motionless, frozen in her fear of fears. Her eyes found him. She was lost. She knew it. He knew it. She slowly lifted the hem of her angel's robe and looked down at her bare feet.

"No socks. No socks," she kept mumbling softly.

He, too, was speaking softly. "The magic's in you. The magic's in you," over and over. Her eyes found his again. Everyone else disappeared into a blurry shadow. Just like all the times it was just the two of them. She was still speaking softly. Instead of "no socks" she was saying, "Not socks. Not socks. Tell the story. Not socks. Tell the story!"

She smiled her impish smile, the one that spoke a thousand words. The one that covered her face every time he asked her to sing. He sat back in his seat. Some great magic was about to happen.

Katie whirled on the ball of one bare foot. The silence was shattered by the sound of her bare feet running on the hardwood stage.

"Get up! Get up!" she yelled as she ran toward the shepherds who were now frozen, not knowing what to do with this change in script.

"The most wonderful thing is about to happen. You're

gonna miss it. The Baby Jesus is about to be born. It's the greatest thing that will ever happen. His mom and dad are in Bethlehem, just around the corner. Don't be scared. God sent me to get you. He wants you to be there. It's real important. It's not far."

Everyone — the shepherds, the audience - was stunned. She was running around the shepherds pulling on their arms, trying to lift them up, pushing them forward. Trying her best to herd them, and their sheep, toward Bethlehem just around the corner.

"C'mon! C'mon, it's the coolest thing ever. You gotta hurry. Tell everyone you see. And if you see some old guys with beards and towels wrapped around their heads carrying packages, bring them too. Let's go! Let's go!" Then she smacked the shepherd leader on the butt, an admonition to get going.

Her excitement spread like wildfire. The audience roared and laughed and clapped thunderously as the "most important angel" led the way to Bethlehem, just around the corner. His face, the girls' too, beamed with pride and amazement.

Mary held the Baby Jesus, gently swaying with the heavenly bundle in her arms, back and forth, back and forth. Joseph, the shepherds with their cotton-ball sheep, and the old guys with beards and towels wrapped around their heads, watched silently. And in the silence, the most important angel appeared above them all.

She found him once again. Smiled that grin again, closed her eyes, and took a deep, deliberate breath. Without warning, without cue, without accompaniment, she began.

O Holy Night, the stars are brightly shining,

The universe had become very small, very focused, there, standing above the Baby Jesus. Life and living had been reduced to their simplest terms, in the innocence and

48

truth and power of this giant voice from this small girl.

Fall on your knees,

Oh hear the angel voices,

Tears streamed down his cheeks. She was singing for him. And God was singing for everyone.

She had never sung like this before. Never! Her voice covered them all like the thin grey blanket that settles between ridges and mountains at sunset, the day's last breath, just before it slips into the anonymity of night. They were all mesmerized by the magic and majesty of this ten-year-old angel, with no socks.

***

He sat on the top step of their wrap-around front porch. He held a cup of coffee in both hands, steam shimmering upward like smoke from his father's pipe. He was still absorbed by Katie's performance. She had received ovation after ovation, ones that rivaled any he had ever seen.

"Whadda ya doing out here? Aren't you cold?" She sat down beside him.

"No, not really. I was just thinking about how very proud I am of you. You were simply amazing."

She just smiled.

"Sweetie, I'm really sorry about the halo. It was my fault that it wasn't made very well. Will you forgive me?"

"For what?"

"For not being as good as Mom at those kinds of things." His voice was about to break.

She stood up and moved down a few steps so she could look him in the eye.

"We don't want you to be her. We just want you to be you. When I was standing up there tonight, right when my halo fell off, I've never been that scared in my life. Then I saw you. And I could tell what you were saying. And I remembered about the magic. It was true. And it's true for you, too. You have the same kinda magic. But you won't let yours out because you think you have to be Mom. She had magic, but hers was different than yours. Not better, just different."

"I have a present for you. It's not a Christmas present. It's just a special Dad present. Here, open it."

He slowly pulled the taped corners open from the ends of the small box wrapped in Santa Claus paper. On top was a note that read, "I don't need these anymore. The magic's in people." Underneath the note were her magic Christmas socks.

THE ANGEL
OF UNION STATION

THE ANGEL
OF UNION STATION

S am Kennedy had been sitting in the same place, in front of the main door to the boarding platforms at Union Station, for hours. Just looking and sitting, sitting and looking. He watched as people passed on their way to somewhere else. So was he – on his way somewhere else. On his way home for the first time in three years.

He sat perfectly erect – back straight; hips, knees, and ankles at ninety-degree angles. His uniform was virtually unwrinkled, a minor miracle since he had been traveling in it for almost three days now. He took great pride in his appearance. His grandmother, who had lived in their home for most of his life, always said, "A man's appearance is like a mirror; people see the reflection as the truth, even though it may actually be hidden on the other side of the glass. So, be careful what you wear. Always be neat, straight, and clean. It goes a long way." He had taken her advice to heart at an early age.

He was a sight to behold. A walking poster for the army. A real-life, honest-to-God war hero, with all the medals and patches and badges to prove it. There was row upon row of ribbons for bravery and conspicuous valor, for being wounded in battle; a Paratrooper Badge, and the Combat Infantryman's Badge. On his sleeve was a round, red patch with a black hourglass in the center - the patch of the Seventh Infantry Division.

He was a strikingly handsome young man. Jet black, wavy hair. Classic facial structure. Six foot two, one hundred and eighty-five pounds. Well, he used to weigh that; he weighed considerably less now. He had big, warm, brown eyes – like those of a cow – eyes that melted the hearts of all the girls he met. The hearts of their mothers, too. These eyes showed his humility, his compassion, his quiet strength. Folks who met him instantly liked him, and felt at ease around him.

Everywhere he went people stared, their eyes drawn to his and to his colorful uniform. He had never gotten used to it, especially now. He felt self-conscious and uncomfortable. He neither thought of himself as handsome nor as a hero. He didn't like attention; had always wanted to be nondescript, which was hard when he was the one everyone wanted to be around. He had hardened some around the edges, but still had the young face.

Sam was twenty-three going on a hundred. He had been thrown into a role far beyond his years, far beyond his imagination. He was lost somewhere between innocence and cynicism, between expectation and resignation, between dreams and dread. He wasn't sure what to feel or think or believe anymore. Mainly, he was tired and alone, and stuck in Union Station in Chicago on Christmas Eve. A long way from Duncan, Oklahoma. A long way from home. And a long way from Jessie.

"Cap'n? Cap'n? You alright?"

Leroy Brookins was a big, barrel-chested black man who was a custodian at Union Station. He always wore bib overalls, with a white shirt and tie underneath. "Just 'cause I's a janitor don't mean I can't look presentable," Brookins (no one called him Leroy) was prone to say. "I wears these overalls 'cause they has lotsa pockets. And they fits my big belly." He wore an old faded fedora. At one time, it was a medium charcoal gray whose brim was neatly blocked. Now it had several black rings just above the band, from years of sweat. He kept it pushed down just above his eyebrows when he was working. But if he stopped to talk, he would always push the brim up to his hairline. "If a man won't let you look him in the eye when he's talkin' to ya, ain't worth wasting you breath. Can't trust 'em. Ain't worth talkin' to."

Brookins, like Sam, was one of those people that everyone warmed up to immediately. His eyes sparkled like stars. His smile was ear-to-ear and showed brilliantly white teeth, with one gold tooth right in the middle.

"'Scuse me for sayin' so, Cap'n, but you sho' is a long ways away. Is somp'n the matter?"

"This was to be my first Christmas home in three years. I was going to ask my girl to marry me. Don't have a ring yet. I don't have much of anything, really."

Sam was to have caught the 8:40 p.m. train to Oklahoma City the night before, but an unexpected and heavy snowstorm had delayed all transportation across the Great Plains. Nothing was going west out of Chicago. Sam had called Jessie's mother and left a message. He had been in Union Station since noon the day before. He had no idea when he would get home. He kept telling himself, "What's a few more days, after all you've been through? Jessie'll be there when you get there."

Brookins sat down beside Sam on one of the arched, double-sided passenger benches. He leaned back against it, pushed the brim of his hat back, and clasped his hands on top of his giant belly.

"How long she been your girl?"

"Since the ninth grade. She's been my only girl. She'll be my only girl."

"She love you like you love her?"

"Yes, she does. She wrote me every week. Sometimes two or three times. She kept me going. Kept my spirits up. Helped me to see what was important. I carried her picture in the webbing of my helmet liner. Some of her letters, too. And after I got hurt, I read them every day in the hospital. It was like she was my guardian angel."

Jessie was statuesque at six feet and strikingly beautiful. Long blonde hair that fell to the middle of her back, and eyes as blue as the Pacific. She had an infectious laugh and a disarming smile. Any man would have been proud to have been her guy. Sam knew he was lucky.

For some reason, Sam felt an instant kinship with Brookins. As though they shared something of importance; something that helped define who they were.

"Seems to me she loves ya as much as you love her. Love's a great thing. It makes us better than we think we can be. But it brings out the devil in us, too. It makes us do things we wouldn't do most of the time – sometimes good, sometimes not. Take this gold tooth. Had the real one pulled and this gold one put in to try and make a woman like me. Said she really liked shiny things. Thought this would really get her. And with my natural beauty and charm," he chuckled out loud, "how could she resist?"

"So, what happened?"

"Laughed at me. Said I wuz fat and dumb. Said she wouldn't go out with me if I had a mouth full of gold. Cost me a month's pay. Man, the things we do to please women. I got the last laugh, though. Wish I had a dollar for every kid that smiled back at me after I flashed this here golden ornament. Yes, sir, can't buy that kinda joy."

"What happened to the woman?"

"She wuz showing off at some fancy party. Stepped on

the hem of her dress and fell down some steps. Knocked out her front teeth." Brookins was beaming. "Didn't have 'nough money to get 'em fixed, much less to have gold ones put in. Just a big gap, now. Whistles when she talks - a real high pitch, the kind that hurts your ears. The kind that makes dogs howl. Course, when she talks everybody has to look to see where that awful sound's comin' from. Yes, sir, the Lord sho' do work in mysterious ways."

Brookins stood up and pushed his hat back down to his eyebrows. He was still reveling in having been victorious. "Yes, sir, life sho' has a way of making things even," he thought out loud. "Better get back to work. I'll stop by a little later."

And off he went. Not really walking, sort of shuffling and dancing at the same time. It was as if his feet were barely touching the floor. Brookins did indeed stop to check on Sam regularly, each time offering some tidbit of wisdom about life or love or the nature of man. On one occasion, when Sam commented that it wasn't going to be a very good Christmas, Brookins allowed, "Seems to me Christmas is 'bout lightin' the darkness. There's light in your life now. Not that terrible darkness you wuz in overseas. The wonderful girl you talk about all the time will be with you sooner than you think. I see how your face lights up when you think of her. Yes, sir, Cap'n, Christmas is 'bout being in the light. 'Bout Jesus light."

Minutes seemed like days. The hours drug by. As they did, Union Station increasingly became more and more deserted. The station was like a banquet room in a castle. Ornate trimmings, intricate inlays in the marble floors. Giant chandeliers hung from the ceiling in succession up and down corridors that seemed to go on forever.

Sam had kept his vigil directly in front of the main exit to the loading platforms. There was a cardboard sign someone had put directly above the doors. It had an arrow pointing out and simply read, "Home." For a day and a half, he had watched throngs of people come in and out of those doors on their way home. Many spoke to him as they passed. It was like he was the gatekeeper; someone whose permission was needed to pass through the doors. Most smiled. Some spoke. Others – primarily other soldiers and children – stopped to chat for a few minutes. Mostly army talk: "Where were you stationed? What unit were you with? Did you see much action? What's those ribbons stand for?"

One young mother with two young boys smiled and spoke as they walked by. "Your daddy's a soldier like that young man," She had said. The boys stopped, fascinated by all of the stuff on Sam's uniform.

"Hey, mister. How come you're wearing a necklace? Soldiers don't wear necklaces. They're for girls," one said.

The mother apologized for her son, smiled again, then dragged them off by their arms. Sam could hear her admonitions in between the clomps of the boys' heels on the marble floor.

The necklace the boy had referred to was actually two sky-blue cloth ribbons that circled his neck and fastened in the back. In the front, just below the knot of his tie, they formed a square. The square was covered with tiny white stars. Below the stars hung a gold circle with a gold eagle in the center. It was the only medal he wore.

Although he had spent most of his time in the station seated, he occasionally walked around to stretch his legs. Sitting for long periods of time made them hurt worse than normal. But he felt self-conscious because he walked with a pronounced limp. He wasn't embarrassed or ashamed; he just didn't want to draw attention to himself. He had been wounded several times. Fortunately, most of the scars were hidden under his uniform.

Sam had spent last Christmas at Walter Reed Army Hospital, convalescing from his most recent injury. The two before that were spent in the Kumwa and Chorwan Valleys along the thirty-eighth parallel. He was just now coming home. What had helped him recover at a fast pace was the thought of spending the next Christmas with Jessie, and with his family. Not at Walter Reed again. No, he was going to be with Jessie on Christmas Eve. And he would ask her to be his wife. All of that energy and discipline and pain dedicated to being home by Christmas Eve, only to be snowbound in Chicago. Where he was lost; where he was really alone. Where he knew no one – except Leroy Brookins.

"Tell me something, Leroy. How long have you been a custodian here?"

"Now, Cap'n, I told you not to call me Leroy. Only them that ain't my friends, or bill collectors, call me that. My friends calls me Brookins. You's my friend ain't ya?"

"Yes. Sorry."

"First off, I's a janitor. Don't know nutin' 'bout being no custodian. Janitors scrub toilets. That's what I do. Guess I been working here 'bout thirty-five years. Yeah, that's right. Came here right when I got out of the army in nineteen-eighteen. Kinda like you, I s'pose."

"So, you were in the first big one."

"Yup. Saw lots of action. Men dying everywhere sometimes. Made some great friends, though. Still keep in touch with some of 'em. Even after all this time. War's a lot like love in some ways. Makes you do things you never thought you could. Some things you never thought of. Some good, some bad. It will change you forever."

Sam was shaking his head in agreement and remembering as Brookins spoke.

"Take that medal around your neck. Bet you never thought you'd ever have anything like that."

"No, Brookins, I never thought that I'd have something like this. I don't think of myself as a hero. I just tried to save my men. They were my responsibility. We were all boys. I wasn't very brave. I was just really scared. Scared for them and scared for me. I was afraid I'd never see Jessie again. That drove me."

"See what I mean about love and war? They's a lot alike, Cap'n. A lot alike."

"Brookins, is there a restaurant close by that might be open? I'm really hungry."

"Well, Cap'n. Let me see. Most places gonna be closed by now. There's the Embers, though. It's real swanky. I hear tell the food's real good, especially the steaks."

"A good steak sounds great. Is it close by? I don't walk very well. What time do you get off? Won't you be my guest for dinner? My treat."

Brookins was visibly moved by Sam's offer. He had only known Sam for a day – and he wasn't used to being invited to dinner at fancy restaurants, especially by white people.

"Thank you very kindly, Cap'n, for you offer. But I better stay right here." Not wanting to embarrass Sam after his generous offer, Brookins said nothing about the fact that he would not be permitted in the Embers Restaurant. "Once things get moving again, it'll be hopping around here. I gots to be ready..."

Sam knew this was an excuse for something else, but didn't want to press the issue. "Brookins, do you have big plans tonight? Gonna see if you can find that woman with the gap between her teeth?" Sam grinned really wide. "Wonder what it's like to kiss a gaped-tooth woman?"

Brookins was grinning, too. "Don't know. Never got close enough to find out. No, sir, I'll be right here all night. Don't know when I'll go home. I have a cot in the store-room. Got a radio. There's an easy chair and a lamp to read by. Got toilet articles, too. I stays here a lot."

"You mean you live here?"

"Sorta. I have a house. Small, but nice. Don't go there much. Ain't nobody there but me. There's always people here at the station, and there's always sump'n to do. Helps fight the loneliness."

Sam didn't know quite how to respond. He just simply said, "I understand." He knew about loneliness.

Sam walked the three blocks to the Embers Restaurant. He really didn't walk; it was more of a step with his left leg and drag his right leg. The Chicago wind was living up to its reputation. He had no overcoat, just his uniform jacket. He was nearly frozen when he got there. Brookins was right. It was a very nice, upscale place. He slowly descended the flight of steps, one at a time, careful not to slip. That would be all he'd need – to end up in another hospital. Remembering his grandmother's instructions, he made sure everything was aligned and in its proper place before he opened the big oak door. Through the cut-glass panels he could see several people waiting to be seated. *Might as well wait here, since I have nowhere else to go*, he thought to himself. *It'll be a nice change from the train station.*

"Good evening, Captain Kennedy. Will there be one for dinner this evening, sir?" The maitre d' was good. He had already surveyed Sam's nametag and rank by the time Sam had approached the podium.

"Yes, I'll be dining alone."

"I'll seat you now." Before Sam could say anything, he was escorted to a corner table that overlooked Michigan Avenue and the lake. As he carefully made his way to the table, men shook his hand and women reached out to touch his arm. It was their way of saying welcome. No one seemed upset that he had walked in off the street and been seated immediately. Everyone smiled as he walked by.

The table was covered with a fine linen tablecloth and set with fine china, silver, and crystal. He couldn't figure out what all the extra forks and spoons were for, though. He was an Oklahoma farm boy; he wasn't used to this. The menu had things on it he had never seen, things he couldn't pronounce. And it was expensive. *Boy, I'm sure a long way from Duncan. If only Jessie could be here*, he thought to himself. He began missing her more.

As people finished their dinner, they all came by his table to shake his hand, or welcome him home, or wish him a merry Christmas. He wasn't sure why. Maybe it was because he was the only person in uniform, or because it was Christmas Eve. Maybe it was the medal around his neck. That thing had gotten him more attention than he liked. He didn't really know, but he had to admit that it made him feel better.

About halfway through his filet, he sat straight back in his chair. He suddenly remembered that he had given the shoeshine man a big tip, more than the shine itself cost. *Oh, no! I'll bet I don't have enough to pay for dinner! I'll get to spend Christmas either in jail or washing dishes*, he thought, neither of which sounded very appealing but wouldn't surprise him. He finished his dinner as best he could. The waiter kept refilling his water glass and coffee cup. It was nice to have coffee that wasn't like black molasses. He was convinced that some of the stuff the army called coffee really came out of tank transmissions. It was hot, though, which helped a little on those awful Korean winter nights.

He had sat there enjoying the atmosphere long enough.

It was time to confess his freeloading. He motioned for the maitre d'.

"Yes, Captain Kennedy, how may I assist you?"

"I need to discuss my check. It seems I've ma—"

Before Sam could confess his sin, the maitre d' interrupted, "You have no check, sir. Do you see the couple at the table by the piano? That's the Bellamys. They are paying for your meal."

"They don't know me. Why would they do that?" Sam was relieved to know that, regardless of the reason, he wouldn't have to add dishpan hands to his list of battle scars.

"Our policy is that no person in uniform pays for his meal. Whomever is next to be seated after the serviceman pays for his dinner. All of our patrons know this and are happy to do it. If we don't recognize someone, then we explain the policy to them. If they don't agree, then they won't be seated. We will continue this policy until the war is over. Please accept your dinner with Mr. and Mrs. Bellamy's compliments."

Sam didn't know quite what to say or do. He had noticed that the Bellamys had periodically looked his way. Now he knew why. At that moment, the couple approached his table. They expressed their gratitude for his service and duty, saying they were honored to have had him as their guest for dinner. They inquired about his home and family, and other pleasantries. He explained that he was snowbound. He said he missed Jessie. They asked him to join them for dessert, which he graciously declined. He thanked them for their generosity. They held his hands warmly as they wished him a quick trip home. They said goodbyes and returned to their table.

He was overwhelmed by their warmth and kindness, and their sincerity to a perfect stranger. "This truly is

Christmas," he muttered out loud.

He stood, straightened his uniform, and placed his hat under his left arm so his right one would be free to assist him up the steps. He made sure that the blue ribbons and the gold eagle were perfectly placed, then began to make his way to the door. And as he did, everyone in the restaurant stood and clapped. Just as before, they touched his sleeve or shook his hand and thanked him as he passed by.

Because he could not walk very quickly, he had taken only a few steps when he stopped dead in his tracks. He stood frozen, staring straight at the entrance. There, standing by the maitre d', was an angel. His angel. Jessie. Sensing that something was wrong, the crowd ceased clapping and stood in silence and stared at Sam. Like Moses parting the Red Sea, the maitre d' waved his arms and those standing between Sam and Jessie made a pathway.

They had not seen each other for over three years. She had not seen how badly he limped. Or the scar across the back of his left hand. Or the one over his left eyebrow. Jessie ran to him. She fell into his arms, kissed his scar, wiped away his tears, and said, "Captain Samuel Kennedy, I love you!"

Tears were flowing now. All Sam could do was hold her as tightly to him as possible, afraid that if he let go he would dissolve into a puddle on the floor around her feet. "Jessica Montgomery, will you marry me?" "Yes! Yes! Yes!"

The applause thundered and cheers rang out as they stood and held each other, alternately crying and laughing.

"How'd you get here?"

"Mr. Brookins brought me. He's standing right outside."

They both turned – but he was not there.

"How'd you get to Chicago?"

"As soon as Mom told me, I took my savings out of the bank. I was determined that we were not going to be apart, not this year. Not because of some stupid snow storm; not after all you've been through. Not this time.

"Daddy drove me to Oklahoma City, where I took the bus to Memphis and then to Lexington. Then a train from Lexington to Chicago, with stops at every little town in Illinois. I thought I'd never get here. When I didn't find you, I just sat down on the bench right inside the main entrance and sobbed.

"Then the voice of an angel spoke my name. 'Miss Jessie, I know where Cap'n Sam is. I'll take you there.' I looked up, and all I saw at first was this giant smile with a gold tooth.

"'Miss Jessie, I'm Brookins. I's been watchin' out for your young cap'n. You feel like walking a short distance? Come on, I'll take you to him. All he done for two days is talk 'bout you. You're a lucky girl. I know you ain't seen him in a long time. He has trouble walkin' good, so you be real gentle with him.

"Then he took my hand, pulled me up, and off we went. It was like magic. I don't remember getting there. It was like he snapped his fingers and there you were. I asked him to come in, but he wouldn't. He said it was our time and he'd see us later."

They stood, hugging and kissing, for what seemed like hours, and all the while everyone in the restaurant kept standing and clapping. Finally, it was time to go.

The maitre d' shook Sam's hand, opened the door, and said, "Thank you, Captain Kennedy, for being our guest on Christmas Eve. And thank you, miss, for giving us all a special gift. Please have a safe journey. Merry Christmas. God bless you."

Sam managed a 'Merry Christmas' and a 'thank you.'

Jessie took him by the arm to help him up the steps, but mostly just to touch him. As they walked back to Union Station, the applause still rang in his ears. The words of the maitre d' and the Bellamys rolled around in his mind. He had gone there alone and empty, and had left filled to over-flowing.

No cars were on the streets, which were still mostly covered with snow. The sky was so clear that it was more blue than black. Like millions of Christmas tree lights, the stars acknowledged those below as they blinked their approval from their celestial posts. Sam began to reflect upon how miracles happened in the strangest places and at the most unexpected times.

***

Union Station was virtually deserted, except for those who had to be there to help others get to where they were going. Like Leroy Brookins. Sam hadn't seen him since their return from dinner. Before, Brookins had been omni-present. Where was he? Sam missed him. He wanted to thank him.

They sat in Sam's familiar spot – the bench in front of the main doors to the tracks. Jessie sat as close to him as she could, almost in his lap. She slid both of her arms around his right arm, then laid her head on his shoulder, and smiled. Sam stared at the sign above the door. Home. "I know it's not Duncan, but this sure feels like home," Sam whispered to Jessie.

"I know," she said. "I know." And they both drifted off to sleep.

***

"Cap'n. Miss Jessie. Ya'll better wake up now. Your train'll be leaving soon. I done loaded your baggage. Eve-

65

rything's been took care of. I saw to it personal. You gonna be home on Christmas after all."

When Brookins spoke, it was with uncommon clarity. His voice commanded attention, but it was always soothing and comforting. It was like the voice of a wise, old grandfather.

They both sat up, moved their heads and necks to get out the kinks. Jessie stood and straightened her clothes, then reached down to help Sam. Brookins looked just like he had the first time Sam saw him.

"Mr. Brookins, I can't thank you enough for watching over Sam for me, and for taking me to him last night," Jessie said sweetly. "You will always have a special place in my heart." She put her arms around him as far as she could and hugged him tightly.

Sam wasn't good with words. "Brookins, you've taught me more than you'll ever know; especially about Christmas, and about loving and life. I will never forget you."

Spontaneously, Sam reached around his neck, unhooked the blue cloth ribbons, and placed his medal around Brookins' neck. "This is the best I have. I want you to have it. Merry Christmas."

Brookins just stood there, his eyes filled with tears. Speechless. He reached in the side pocket of his overalls and pulled out a rectangular box about six inches long and four inches wide. It was wrapped in bright red paper.

"Cap'n Sam, you wuz nicer to me than anyone has been in a long time. I wants you to have this. Don't know anybody else has 'nough love to give it to. But you can't open it till the train is outta the station." He put it in Sam's hand and bear-hugged him.

"All aboard!" The conductor's voice signaled that it was time to go.

Brookins put one arm around each of them. "You kids get goin' now." Jessie kissed him on the cheek and Sam shook his hand, then they boarded the train.

Sam was both anxious and excited about opening Brookins' gift. He unwrapped one corner and slid the red paper off. It was a black, hinged box; one he had seen many times. He opened it from the bottom. There was a gold circle with a gold eagle in the center. The circle was attached to two ribbon-like pieces of sky-blue cloth. The citation read: "For conspicuous valor while in the face of imminent danger, without regard for personal safety...the Congress of the United States of America awards this Medal of Honor to Leroy L. Brookins."

Sam's hands were shaking. Jessie reached over, took the box from him, and put her hand on his. "Isn't this just like the one you gave Mr. Brookins?" Sam just nodded. Jessie took the medal out of the box and clasped it around Sam's neck.

They rode in silence for awhile; Sam holding the box and citation, Jessie holding Sam's hands, occasionally gently rubbing the scar.

"Sammy, do you believe that angels actually watch over us? This whole time, I've felt like someone was watching over me and guiding me to you. And when I saw you, I knew it."

"I didn't used to, Jess. But I do now," Sam replied, squeezing her hand. "One of them lives in Union Station."

OUR STAR

OUR STAR

As he lay in bed collecting his senses, he noticed how the light shining through the blinds made stripes of black and white on the hardwood floor. There was no graying around the edges, but a clear distinction where one stopped and the other began. It occurred to him that we tend to color life all of the time with bright splashes and subtle hues; that somehow, life was unclear, the truth uncertain, unless it was viewed in living color.

I'm like that he thought. *I guess most of us are. But how often do we miss significant moments in our lives because we're looking for something bigger or brighter or more important? How often do we fail to realize that life really is very simple – we are the ones to make it complicated? And more than we realize, the important things are in the truth of black and white.*

He was feeling very guilty because he had been gone from home a lot; not out of town, just working. He had been jerked and pulled in many different directions by many different sources, all of which seemed important, at least to him. All of the meetings at night, the extra work on the weekends, the things that other people asked him to do gave him a sense of self-worth and made him feel important, which was something he needed very badly. He had become quite an accomplished juggler and magician and tight-rope walker.

He was really looking forward to Christmas this year. It was going to be a fun time with his family, especially with his kids. Most of his contact with them lately had been notes pinned to his underwear, or smiley faces drawn on sticky notes stuck all over the dashboard of his car. For all he knew, the kids were probably off in college or married or in prison by now, a fate that he and his wife had discussed on more than one occasion regarding one child in particular. But since he had not been contacted by the police, lawyers, or the parents of pregnant girls, he assumed that all was at least what he expected on the home-front.

After realizing that it was Saturday morning and he didn't have to get up at any particular time, he lay back in the bed and began to soak up the Saturday morning environment. *Ah, yes*, he thought, *what a great feeling this is, just to lie here and relax.*

As he lay there, piled up in mounds of covers and pillows, he wistfully flashed back through the years to a simpler time; a time when Saturday mornings were filled with the sounds of his children running through the house playing hide-and-seek; the greasy, salty smell of bacon frying; the aroma of freshly ground coffee that would serpentine through the house; the clatter of pots and pans banging together as they were being put away. It was a time filled with play, a time when the only chauffeuring he had done was on his hands and knees, hauling little ones to tea parties. A time when life was far less jammed and disjointed.

He was jolted back to reality by a dull *thud-thud-thud*, like a bowling ball might make as it rolled from stair to stair to stair. Just as quickly came what had to be the sounds of an ax murder occurring at the bottom of the stairs.

"Ah-eeee! Ah-eeee!" screamed the youngest of his four children.

How can that noise come from such a small, five-year-old body? he thought, waiting to see what awful noise would shake the windows next. And what he heard was clearly the sound of some serial killer satisfied with his handiwork.

"Aaa-ha, ha, ha, haaa!" rang through the house in such a sinister fashion that Vincent Price would have been proud.

He thought, *There's no way that child came from me. Obviously, there's a recessive, psychotic gene in his mother's family that is manifesting itself in my house in the form of an eight-year-old boy.*

The screams of terror became interspersed with, "Mommy, Mommy! Jason pulled me down the steps. And I didn't do anything to him at all. I was just sitting there. And he grabbed me and pulled my feet and I hit my head on all thirty-seven steps."

"She did too!" came the self-righteous retort, to ensure that Mom knew that the impromptu lobotomy he had just performed on his sister was completely justified. "I was just walking by and she made this ugly face at me. And it hurt my feelings. And anyway, I didn't pull her down the stairs; she tripped and did that herself."

Then the ever-so-familiar sibling dialogue commenced.

"I did not trip! You pulled me!"

"You did too trip!"

"Did not!"

"Did too!"

"Did not!"

"Did too!"

This exchange usually went on for days, or at least until some much bigger person interceded, or another innocent victim became the focus of Jason's one-track little brain. As he continued to listen, their exchange became more distant, a clear sign that they had either been summoned to the great, wise arbiter in the kitchen, or that Jason had stuffed her half-dead little body in a garbage bag and was dragging his cumbersome cache to bury it under the porch, leaving trails of guts and goo, something he had threatened her with before.

***

Today was decorate-the-Christmas-tree day. Aside from watching the kids open their presents, decorating the tree was his most favorite thing to do at Christmas. It was the one thing in which all family members participated. Each had their own assigned duties, determined more by stature than interest. Popcorn and cranberries would be strung into long strands of white and burgundy beads. Lights would be placed with such precision that any illumination expert would be proud. The collection of homemade ornaments – snowmen with moveable arms and legs, paper stars with four or five or eight points, blue and green and orange cloth Christmas trees with buttons for ornaments (created at church and school) – all would be placed with love and care in the most conspicuous places on the tree. This usually meant the distribution of ornaments was less than even; more in bunches, also a function of stature or whomever got there first. The silver slivers of icicles would be draped two or three at a time to ensure that the whole tree dazzled in kaleidoscopic brilliance.

And there was the star: the one he had made as a boy, the one that had adorned every Christmas tree he could remember. It was made of cardboard covered with white felt. The edges were traced in not-so-straight lines of gold glitter, with incongruous flecks of gold scattered all over the star. It was a big star; a really big star. Fortunately, his family – both as a boy and now – had always had a large tree, so it never looked too big for the tree. At least he had never thought so.

Over the years, it had been re-felted, re-glued and re-glittered more times than he could remember. It was creased around the edges and smudged in places, but it was still, to him, the most beautiful thing on the tree. It had a special quality. It seemed to create light rather than reflect it. Maybe it was because of all the scattered glitter, or the white felt. He didn't know. He just knew that it seemed to glow on its own.

***

He roamed through the house searching for signs of life. All was quiet. Too quiet. *Maybe Jason has met his match, and they are all out scattering his remains over some toxic waste dump,* he though, smiling. *Nah! Never happen.*

He heard the faint sounds of live bodies down in the den. A trail of dolls, shoes, coats and cars led the way to where he could find them. *God only knows what they're doing. And what I'll find when I open the door.* But since he didn't hear whimpers or chainsaws, it was probably safe to go in.

There they were; his whole family. All five of them. They weren't doing anything together, but at least they were all in one place. Jennifer was doing the thing all six-teen-year-old girls do best – talking to some boy on the phone. Jeff was watching *Wrestle Mania,* something most thirteen-year-old boys had enough brain cells to do. Jill was untying several pairs of shoes whose laces had been tied together.

"Who tied all of your shoes together?"

"Jason," came their unanimous response.

"Where is Daddy's little future felon?" he quipped.

At that instant, Jason flashed by with a large pair of

scissors in his hand. "Here, Killer! Here, boy!" Jason called as he headed out of the room.

Killer was the tabby cat Jason had found (stole was more like it) on his way home from school one afternoon. It was obvious who had named the cat. For some time, Jason had tried to trim his name in Killer's fur. His reasoning, he said, was so that if Killer ever got lost, then whomever found him would know who he belonged to. So far, Jason had only managed to trim sort of a "J" in Killer's fur.

I probably ought to stop him, he thought to himself. *No, it's okay. Killer is quicker than he is, most of the time. He can scamper up a tree. And besides, better the cat than one of us.*

All of the Christmas tree decoration boxes were scattered around the room, their contents organized in various piles. It was clear which pile was his – the thousands and thousands of lights, enough to direct air traffic at Atlanta International Airport.

"Alright everybody. It's time to decorate the tree. Jennifer, tell the boyfriend du jour to call you back. You won't die for the next few hours. And be sure that he calls you! You don't call him." (He was still old-fashioned about some things, especially where she was concerned.) "Jill, you go find Jason. No, wait. You stay here! Jeff, you go find Jason."

"Aw, Dad. Why do I have to? He's such a dork!"

"You're bigger than he is; you can beat him up. And he's not a dork."

"Yes, he is a dork," his wife chimed in, without looking up from testing the exponential number of tree lights.

"Okay. He's a dork. But he's still your brother."

"It's not my fault he's my brother. Now I know why wild animals eat their young."

"You're right. It's your mother's and my fault he's here."

Just then, he caught the look from Carol. It was an it's-your-fault-not-mine-you-caught-me-in-a-moment-of-weakness-I-accept-no-responsibility look.

"But what if he still has the scissors?"

"Then jump on him and trim your name in his hair. I'm sure that Killer would like that. I don't care. Just get him back in here. Jennifer, I asked you to get off the phone."

"Just a minute, Dad. I'm almost through."

"No, now. We need to get started."

"Just a minute!"

No sixteen-year-old is going to talk to me like that, he thought. He calmly went over to where she was sitting, took the receiver from her hand, and said in his deepest voice, "I'm sorry, Fred or Ralph or George or whatever your name is. Jennifer has to go now. Her husband just got out of jail and she has to change the baby's diapers. Thank you for calling." Then he hung up.

She was mortified! Words failed her. Actually, a lot of words came to mind, but none she dared say to her father. She glared at him. He glared at her. It was clear to both that grounding was imminent. Not wanting to be sentenced to Devil's Island, where there was no phone and no boys, she opted to say nothing.

During this little father-daughter chat, his wife had managed to check the forty-three strands of lights. She had laid them end-to-end, to make sure that no two colors were in succession, and that the blinking sequence did not create a strobe-light effect. The red, green, blue, orange, and white flashing neon snake wound its way at least to the next town.

Where did we ever get all of these lights? The kids must have been selling them for the PTA. And how will I ever get them all on the tree? he puzzled, trying to decide the best logistics to accomplish this lighting lunacy. He had learned the hard way that he had no directorial authority, no veto power. His role was simply to follow someone else's instructions.

Jason was the designated electrician's helper. It was something the little heathen could do and not wreak too much terror on everyone else. It also kept him from trying to pierce Jill's ears with ornament hangers.

He unplugged the strands of lights and carefully rolled them into ovals for easier handling. Jill was sitting patiently, waiting to begin light placement instruction. He heard the clomping of two big feet and two little feet coming down the stairs to the den. Jennifer was still fuming, sitting on the couch with her arms folded across her chest so tightly that her fingers had turned white. Just as he stood up in the chair to start putting the lights on the tree, Jeff appeared with Jason in tow, the former looking the worse for the wear.

"Jason, come over here and help Daddy put the lights on the tree. Now, don't do anything until I tell you. Okay? You three start getting the ornaments ready."

"But I wanted to go shoot ball!"

"This stuff is for the little brats to do. Anyway, I'm still mad at you. And besides, you're not even close to being ready to put the ornaments on."

These were the responses he got from the older two.

"First, you're not going to shoot ball until we're finished. Second, I know that neither of you two thinks it's cool to do things with the family. Most importantly, this is a family tradition; something you'll remember fondly when you get to be ancient like me."

The frustration left his voice. He understood they wanted to do something else. He stepped down and sat in the chair.

"This is an important time for all of us. It's an important time for me. Most days, we're running in a million different directions. We're like ships that pass in the night. I know I'm worse than anyone. I feel like I'm losing you, if I haven't lost you already. The little ones will be gone in a blink, then it will be just your mom and me. And we won't be the most important people in your lives anymore. I have trouble dealing with that. Try to understand. It's not just decorating the tree, it's the process. It's something we always do together."

Silence.

He had assumed his words would fall on deaf ears. The younger ones wouldn't understand, and the older ones didn't care. Jennifer and Jeff went back to the couch to wait for their sentences to be carried out. Jill waited quietly, as she always did. Jason began collecting the ovals of lights. He stood in the chair and began carefully clipping the lights in ever-increasing circles. No one was having any fun, himself included. This was not turning out like it was supposed to.

"Jason, hand Daddy some more lights," he said, reaching behind him with one hand and continuing to place lights with the other, a talent acquired from years of practice.

"Jason, hand me some more lights. Jason, what are you doing?" He turned to see what the problem was.

"No, son! Don't plug the lights in. You'll shock yourself!"

Too late. There Jason stood, like a spool of thread, wound from head to toe in every strand of lights. Glowing in red and blue and green flashing brilliance; smiling from ear-to-ear and full of himself.

"Don't move, son. Just stand still. I'll get down and get you out of that mess before you get burned."

"But I want Mommy to see me. She'll like it."

"No, you don't! She'll kill us both. Why didn't one of you two stop him? He could have really hurt himself."

"Are you kidding?" one replied. "If he's dumb enough to be a human light bulb, then he deserves what he gets."

After unplugging young Tom Edison, and after all the lights were finally placed on the tree, the tradition was to allow the children to hang the ornaments and icicles. Amid under-their-breath comments, the big kids took the top; the little kids attacked the bottom. Jennifer and Jeff finished in world-record time, and then vanished without a word. He wasn't really paying much attention anymore, just staring blankly at the tree. He wanted to get it done.

***

He had fallen asleep in the chair. The chair wasn't really his chair; at least he had never said so. But it was the most comfortable chair in the house, and everyone knew to get out

of it when he came in. He was convinced that the fabric was treated with some invisible, odorless drug that invaded his body through osmosis and put him to sleep. It never failed.

When he awoke, the room was dark. Everyone was gone. He hoped that all had completed their assignments so he wouldn't have to finish it by himself. He plugged in the lights to critique their work. Except for the icicles, the top half looked very nice; in fact, it was rather pretty. The bottom half was another story.

Three or four bottom limbs were heavily laden, each bowed from the weight of seventeen ornaments. The higher limbs were sparsely decorated, or not at all. The ornaments were hung in succession, like little toy soldiers lined up in Christmas formation. They had been placed with great care and precision and love, with an obvious effort to make the tree as beautiful as possible.

The icicles were a different matter. They had been somewhat carefully hung in groups of five or six on the limbs Jason could reach. He had actually done a pretty good job, certainly better than usual. How he had placed the icicles on the top half of the tree was the problem. Shiny silver wads adorned it. Their arrangement was the result of where they had come to rest among the flashing lights and cloth dollies, having been heaved heavenward a glob at a time.

He reached to un-wad a clump of icicles hanging like a silver ornament on the most eye-catching limb, then stopped short. *No, they took great care to do this. This was their job. I'm not going to rearrange anything this year. The tree is beautiful just the way it is.*

As he stood there, something shining in his peripheral vision caught his eye. It was the star; lying on the table, waiting for the master to put it in its place. With great deliberation and tenderness, he stood up in a chair and gently hung the star on the very top of the tree. Then he stepped down to view the whole tree from farther back in the room.

It was a gorgeous tree, even with all the decoration gaps on the bottom branches. It seemed to have a perfect triangular, stair-step shape. Each light and ornament dazzled in its own right, but each led the way to the top – to the old, big star.

In his mind he raced through tree after tree after tree, his hallmarks of family togetherness, and the guardians of his innocence. The star always glowed more than he remembered. There was always a distinct difference in its appearance when it was finally in place. It always looked brand-new. No dirt. No bent edges. Just as bright and wonderful as when he made it, thirty-five years ago. Its transformation transcended time and space. It drew from him, from anyone who saw it, all the best of what he was, and then filled the room with celestial light. Life became clear – as clear as a Persian night with a similar star.

"Isn't it a beautiful star, Daddy?" The tiny voice spoke, unsure if he was still sleeping. "It's an old star and it's kinda beat up, but it shines so much brighter than the other lights on the tree."

"And see how its light makes all the other ornaments sparkle? And how it lights up the dark places in the tree? You know, the places where Jill and I didn't do such a good job," said another small, unexpected voice.

"It's almost like all the other lights are plugged into that one old star at the very top," Jill said, beaming.

"Just looking at it sure does make all our hard work worth it," Jason said with pride.

From the darkness, older voices echoed the theme. "Ooh, what a beautiful tree, Daddy. Now that I think about it, it was sorta fun to decorate. Kinda like it's always been."

"Yeah, it does look pretty cool. I guess I really didn't want to shoot ball anyway."

"Honey, it's the best, most beautiful tree ever," Carol said completing the family chorus.

Jason perched on his knee, legs stretching to touch the floor. Jill climbed into his lap and leaned back against his chest.

"Daddy?"

"Yes, sweetheart."

"I think your star is just as pretty as the star that led the shepherds and wise men to baby Jesus. And I think that if we threw your star way up in the sky, and if Jesus was born tonight, it would lead us right to Him with ab-so-lute-ly no trouble," Jill said confidently.

"My Sunday school teacher says that Jesus was the light of the world. I guess kinda like your star," Jason said, wanting confirmation of his insight.

"I think you are ab-so-lute-ly right, son. And I think you are both very smart."

Jill snuggled closer, put her arms around his neck, and kissed him on the cheek. She got face-to-face with him and said, "I love you, Daddy. Merry Christmas."

His vision was filled with her face silhouetted in front of the star.

"I love you too, sweetheart."

"I sure do love our tree. And I sure do love your star."

"No, sweetheart, it's our star. It's our star."

YOU'VE DONE ENOUGH

YOU'VE DONE
ENOUGH

He had never quite learned that trying to be all things to all people almost always meant that he was nothing to anyone.

Christmas was a double-edged sword. The joy he felt in giving seemed to always be played off by his feelings of inadequacy. There were always more people to do for than he had time or money to accomplish. He felt a strange sense of guilt, because he had a comfortable life when there were always thousands immediately around him that had little or nothing.

He always encouraged his children, especially at Christmas, to survey their toys and clothes they rarely used and give them to charitable causes. They, of course, always found legitimate reasons to hang on to dust-laden toys and too-small clothes. "I may want to play with it sometime," or "I know it's too small; I'm saving it for my children," were typical responses to the requests for closet purging.

"Aren't you being just a little bit selfish, especially when so many kids won't get anything for Christmas?" he would say, in his best father-figure voice. He always avoided saying children who would get nothing for Christmas, because he anticipated what would be the logical response: "But why won't Santa bring them anything, especially if they've been good?" A reasonable question for which he had no answer.

He often wondered why he felt so compelled, so driven to be all things to all people. He genuinely enjoyed doing things for people, but beyond his desire was a deep-seated need; a need that both inspired him and fueled his insecurities. By the same token, his actions were paradoxically complete and incomplete. He always felt good about what he did for others, but he was never satisfied that what he had done was enough.

Growing up, he had seen the countless things his parents had done for others; they had never turned their backs on anyone who needed them. They had never had material things to give, only their time, talent and compassion. Of all the things his father had told him when he was growing up, the one he remembered the most was, "Son, you give what you have and you help who you can." He had carried those words with him always. But for as much comfort and compassion that they created, they were also a curse; feeding his guilt and inadequacy, because there was always someone close by who needed something from him. At Christmas, his father's instructions became sources of frustration and joy rolled into one.

There were times – as he ran the gauntlet from store to store, amid the throngs of grabbers and pushers – that he became paralyzed, unable to get anything done. Going through his mental inventory of matching people with gifts, all against the backdrop of only a few dollars, often became a futile endeavor. At times like those the lists of names matched with items became too much to sort out, especially with all the bell-ringers at every door, and the needy children on every channel. Those times usually cut short the shopping safaris. He would just go home, but always put some money in the bell-ringer's bucket on the way out. And he always told himself, *I'll do better tomorrow.*

***

"Okay, you guys, get your coats on. It's time to become CHRIST-MAS SHOP-PERS!" These words always struck notes of dread for all those within earshot.

"Aw, Dad, do we have to? We want to watch TV," or "I'm too tired," or "I'm not going anywhere with him," were typical responses. Never did they say, "Oh, boy! It's time to go shopping with Father dear. It will be fun just being together." He didn't blame them.

His first line of defense went something like, "Come on, guys, this is the season for giving, for helping those who are less fortunate, for trying to live the way Jesus taught us. Haven't you learned anything I've tried to teach you, or that you've learned in church?" Ah, yes, good old guilt. What would parenting be without it? His experience was that guilt was a great persuader. But add some divine intercession and you had an almost unbeatable combination. This was the first Christmas, however, for a new variable in the parent versus children equation – puberty!

He had forgotten, if he had ever known at all, that along with the arrogance, the sudden shifts in moods, the "I have hormones so I know it all" attitude, that puberty dissolved the adolescent conscience into an "I come first" gooey mess.

But had puberty destroyed the time-honored, "If you aren't good, then Santa will only bring you a lump of coal and a bundle of switches" approach? He doubted that it would work, but the introduction of adolescence into his annual shopping spree called for a more aggressive attack. It was worth a try. He was getting desperate.

Just as he was about to give his best "You better watch out, you better not cry" rendition, he heard one whisper to the other, "Now comes the Santa routine."

He stood there feeling and looking out-smarted. They, on the other hand, sat there with THE LOOK – raised eyebrows, wrinkled nose, tightened mouth. He hated that look; not just because of its condescending appearance, but because it oozed with patronizing pubescent piety. THE LOOK was usually followed by equally ugly comments, such as a flippant "Gah" or "I can't believe it." It was clear that he would have to employ the defense of last resort, what he learned in the army as the final protective fires. In parental terms, "Hit 'em with every ounce of power you have."

By the numbers he assumed the position: left hand on left hip (he was right-handed); weight evenly distributed on both feet; knees slightly bent to avoid passing out (also a trick he learned in the army, the hard way); voice clear and deep; eyes piercing. His body was ready for the coup de gras. With one flick, his right arm was raised perpendicular to his body, his index finger rigid. He stood motionless, like a highly trained hunting dog. His finger was not pointed at either of them, but between them, so that there would be no misunderstanding that the final volley was intended for both. His father's words rang in his ears as he fired the final shot.

"Alright, that's it! Both of you get your money! Put on your coats! We're going shopping! And we're going now! End of discussion!" Ah, spoken like a true father. As a teenager, he had sworn – what he remembered as a daily occurrence – that he would never say that to his own children. So much for the innocence of youth.

As he approached the car, he was besieged by one in tears and the other screaming, "It's my turn to sit up front! She sat up front yesterday!"

"No, I didn't! That was the day before," she retorted between sobs.

"Then it's still my turn! Don't you know anything!
You're so dumb!"

"Well, I want to sit by Daddy!"

"So do I!"

So much for having the last volley.

*Ah, such love for their father; I don't want either of
them up front if it's going to be like that,* he thought.

"Both of you, in the back seat! NOW! I don't want to
hear another word from either of you. Just sit there and
think of how selfishly you've been acting!" Guilt deserved
another try.

The weather was crummy, entirely appropriate for the
events of the day. All had been quiet for a while on the front
lines after the last skirmish. He didn't delude himself that
they were in the back seat doing silent contrition for their
crimes against fatherhood. No, this wasn't silent soul-
searching. This was THE SILENT TREATMENT! The old
I'll-show-him-I-won't-make-a-sound-for-a-week-treatment.

Christmas traffic was always bad, but today it was inor-
dinately terrible. He was convinced that every car owner in
Ohio and Michigan was in front of him. If they weren't in
RVs, then they were pulling campers heading for the balmy
climes in southern Florida. And every driver was at least a
hundred and twenty-five years old. You know the type:
steering wheel grasped tightly with one hand at ten o'clock
and the other hand at two o'clock; barely able to see over
the steering wheel; driving ten miles per hour under the
speed limit, and in the left lane.

They had been sitting in traffic for what seemed to be
twelve days. Some jerk who had been directly in front of
him had decided not to turn from the turn lane, but rather to
merge (stop was more appropriate) back into the flow of
lame-turtles traffic - sort of musical turn signals. No doubt
the car was from Michigan.

Things had become strangely quiet in his car. But then it happened.

"Look over there, Daddy! In that vacant parking lot. See that car?

He had been oblivious to most everything around him. It was a wonder he hadn't slammed into another car. As he looked over at the parking lot, he saw a man about his age leaning against the hood of a very used Ford sedan.

"What does that sign say? It's too dark, I can't see it very well. Can either of you make it out?"

"WILL WORK FOR FOOD," came in unison from the back seat.

"Let's see if we can help those people." Without hesitation, he pulled into the lot.

As he pulled up beside the other car, his daughter acknowledged the two small girls in the back seat, their smudged faces pressed against the window. Their smiles seemed to be connected to each other. Both sets of kids waved. The communication was simple, yet powerful; the kind only children can give and understand.

By the time he had gotten out of the car, the other father was walking toward him. As he approached the other man, he put his hand in his pocket and clasped all the money he had, though not a great sum. The two shook hands. As they did, he slipped the money to the other man. They stood there, motionless, more holding hands than shaking them. No words were spoken. Their eyes said all that was necessary, and in a way that only fathers can understand. Each then turned and got in his car.

He just sat there behind the wheel for a few minutes; tears streaming down his cheeks. Now there were four cherub faces in the back windows, all connected by bigger-than-life smiles.

What he dreaded all night finally hit. *What else can I*

do? Should I go to the bank and get more money? Should I take them to get some food? I've given them all my money. What else is there? As suddenly as his kids had found the car, he began to recite to himself the verse from Luke: "And ye shall find the babe wrapped in swaddling clothes. Lying in a manger." He thought, *A manger can't be much different than the back seat of a broken-down car.*

"Let's not shop tonight, Daddy," came the plea from the back seat. "Let's go home."

"Okay," was all he could utter.

As he began to leave the parking lot, he noticed in his rearview mirror the two small girls smiling and waving. And he noticed that the only street light in the parking lot had now come on and was shining directly above the other car. He stopped the car before he pulled out of the lot. He took a deep breath and wiped his tears from his eyes.

"What's the matter, Daddy," she asked sensitively, knowing that he had been crying.

"I gave those people all of our money, but I don't know if we helped them very much. I just wish I could do more."

There was brief silence. Then his son spoke softly, as he reached across the seat to hug his dad.

"Those people can have a good meal and a warm place to stay tonight because of you. You've done enough for today."

Printed in the United States
90677LV00003B/301-999/A